By SARAH BLACK

NOVELS
The General and the Horse-Lord
The General and the Elephant Clock of Al-Jazari

NOVELLAS
Anagama Fires
Idaho Battlegrounds
Idaho Pride
The Legend of the Apache Kid
Marathon Cowboys
Marlowe's Ghost
Sockeye Love

Published by DREAMSPINNER PRESS
http://www.dreamspinnerpress.com

THE
GENERAL AND THE
HORSE-LORD

SARAH BLACK

Dreamspinner Press

Published by
Dreamspinner Press
5032 Capital Circle SW
Suite 2, PMB# 279
Tallahassee, FL 32305-7886
USA
http://www.dreamspinnerpress.com/

This is a work of fiction. Names, characters, places, and incidents either are the product of author imagination or are used fictitiously, and any resemblance to actual persons, living or dead, business establishments, events, or locales is entirely coincidental.

The General and the Horse Lord
© 2013 Sarah Black.

Cover Art
© 2013 Anne Cain.
annecain.art@gmail.com
Cover content is for illustrative purposes only and any person depicted on the cover is a model.

ISBN: 978-1-62798-837-7
Digital ISBN: 978-1-62798-838-4

Printed in the United States of America
Second Edition
December 2013
First Edition published by Dreamspinner Press, April 2013

PROLOGUE

Kuwait, 1990

"GENERAL, THERE'S a Kuwaiti boy here, says he has a letter for you. Won't give it to anyone else. I frisked him. He's clean, but he won't tell me what he wants. Just says he has a letter for you, and it's life and death."

John looked up at his sergeant. "Can you check on it?" He leaned back over the topo map, drew in the route for the new bridge. "We need to do it here or here," he said, pointing to the penciled alternate. "Otherwise the roadwork will take too long to build."

His chief engineer followed the line of the river. "Where was the old bridge before they blew it?"

John pointed to the trail, marked as a dashed line on the map. "The foundations are gone. They tried to run a tank over it. The tank's still there, but no way can we move it, not with our current equipment."

Sergeant Miller was back. "Sir, you may want to see this kid. He speaks excellent English with a very proper Brit accent. His sandals are torn up from the road, but they were expensive once. He asked for John Mitchel, not General Mitchel. Didn't know your rank."

John looked up, puzzled. "Yeah, okay." He threw a towel over the map. "Send him in here."

The boy was small and thin, maybe eight years old, with dusty black hair and deep circles of fatigue under big, dark eyes. He stepped up, held out his hand to John. "Sir, are you John Mitchel? I am Abdullah al-Salim. I believe you know my father."

John shook his hand. The boy was trembling, shock or pain, maybe both. "Of course I know your father. He's my good friend. I know you as well, though I haven't seen you since you were three, I think, already kicking a soccer ball around the yard. I thought your father had the family back in Cambridge. Sit down and let's get you some water."

"No, not yet. I have to give you the letter."

His lips were cracked and bleeding from the heat, and he was swaying on his feet, his face suddenly pale under the dust. John picked him up and set him down on his lap. He was as frail as a bird. "You eat and drink, and I'll read the letter, okay?" He looked at Miller, and the man nodded, left the tent to get food. Miller had kids. He would know what to bring. "Where's your father? Is he still at your house?"

"He's hiding behind a wall in the basement. The soldiers came looking for him. He sent my mother and sisters to Lebanon, and he sent me to find you." The boy closed his eyes, laid his head down on John's shoulder with a sigh.

John put his arms around the boy. "You're safe now. Just rest, Abdullah."

"Please, will you help him? Sir, I don't think he was planning to come out."

John opened the letter. He recognized the handwriting immediately.

John, my friend.

I must beg your help for my son. The women, they will be safe, but the Iraqis are taking the sons of men like myself, leaving them in shallow graves in the desert. It's a very old technique in war, is it not? It means something different to me today than when we studied together. Please, John, get him out of Kuwait and to safety. He is the very best of me. Don't worry about me. I'm an old man, but my son is filled with beauty and light, and the world needs his light.

Omar.

Miller came in with a bottle of water and a thermos cup of soup. John stood, set the boy down on the desk chair. "Drink some water and eat the soup, then we'll talk. But tell me this, is your father still in Al Jahra? I remember your house had orange trees in front. Is that the one?"

The boy nodded yes, his eyes on the bottle of water. He looked up at Sergeant Miller. "Thank you."

"You're welcome." Miller pulled up a chair. "I'll just sit with you while you eat, son. Are you hurt?"

The boy shook his head. John ducked into the second room of the command tent, spoke to his radio operator. "Balish, can you get CW-3 Sanchez on the radio? I need to know where his squadron is."

"The Horse-Lords? I think they're two klicks down the road, General. Do you need him if he's free?"

"Yes, I do."

Gabriel walked into the command tent ten minutes later, his flight suit dusty. "I've got an Apache fueled up, General." He looked tired, his eyes dark and warm and smiling.

John let himself take a long look. "Sanchez, I need some transpo and backup, but feel free to say no. This is off the books, a little rescue mission into the city. I'll probably get us killed. We've been ordered not to do anything stupid like this."

"Roger that. Congratulations for putting on the star, General."

John smiled at him. "Yeah, a week now. I should enjoy it, because I'm about to lose it." He pulled Gabriel to the back of the tent. The boy was sleeping on his field cot. "This is Abdullah al-Salim. He's the son of an old friend, Dr. Omar al-Salim. Omar was my dissertation advisor at Harvard. We've been friends for years. He taught me Greek, Gabriel."

Gabriel nodded. "Okay, Greek, got it. What do you need?"

John grinned at him. Gabriel never wasted time on the nonessentials. "He's been targeted as an intellectual. He asked me to get his son out of the country. Why don't we go get him, send them both back home to America?"

"Roger that, General. You know where he is?"

"Al Jahra, just west of Kuwait City. In hiding."

"Oh, shit. Heavy tank losses in Al Jahra." Gabriel looked closer at the sleeping boy, reached out and touched his foot. "His feet have been bleeding. Did he walk here barefoot?"

"Sandals."

"Okay, boss. Let me go check the weapons. I'll have to blow the helo if they try to take it. We'll be on foot in the city."

"You got your side arm?" Gabriel nodded. "Let me see what else I can round up."

Gabriel was already moving out of the tent. "I'll find some smoke grenades. Smoke is always good to make a confusing situation a little more confusing."

John checked the ammunition for his side arm, then grabbed two M16s and briefed Miller. "No one comes after me if I fuck this up, Miller."

"Why don't you stay here and I'll go, sir? We really don't want to lose a general officer."

"Negative, Sergeant."

"How long before I sound the alarm?"

"You don't. I don't come back, you get that boy to my sister in Virginia. Any way you can, Miller, understand? His father's got an American passport."

"Roger that, General. No worries. So where are you going?"

"Al Jahra. I'm going to extract Dr. al-Salim and bring him here. I'm taking Sanchez."

Miller nodded. "Okay, well, your odds of survival just went up about 99 percent. We'll give you twelve hours, and then we come after you."

"Negative."

"See you in twelve hours, sir."

Gabriel had set the chopper down on the tarmac beyond the last hanger. John climbed in, shaking his head, and the pilot lifted the helo into the air until they were clear of the makeshift base. "We've got twelve hours. Miller is such a pain in the ass. I gave him a direct order not to come after me and I know he's going to blow it off and bring a frigging tank if we don't show up on time."

"Actually, that makes me feel better. Did you see the new horse on the nose?"

"Yeah. I like that golden mane. Wild. You always have the best art on your birds."

"It's not art. It's the soul of man and machine together. That boy walked here from Al Jahra? That's over thirty miles." Gabriel leaned over, took John by the shirtfront, and pulled him close. John could feel the heat of Gabriel's breath on his mouth. He'd been chewing cinnamon gum. "Are we off to rescue an old boyfriend?"

John smiled up into his eyes for so long Gabriel leaned a tiny bit closer, kissed him hard. John reached for his cheek and ran his fingers over two days of rough stubble. "You're my only old boyfriend. Try not to get killed, okay?"

"I haven't slept with you since you've been promoted. I'd hate to miss sleeping with a general."

"You know we can't let them take a general officer, even just a road-builder like myself. It would be too embarrassing for everyone. If things go south, you'll need to take care of it for me."

"You're saying, what, you want me to shoot you in the head if the bad guys are closing in?"

"Roger that." John wondered if he should tell Gabriel he loved him. No, that would freak him out worse than ordering him to shoot him in the head. John shoved the two rifles down between his knees. Gabriel studied the instrument panel. His mouth was pressed into a thin line.

"Let's get the job done and get through this night, pilot, and I'll treat you to a bottle of tequila. And anything else you'd like."

Gabriel looked at him, an unwilling smile softening his mouth. "Anything?"

THE GENERAL AND THE HORSE LORD

CHAPTER 1

GENERAL JOHN MITCHEL was not a happy man. He flipped through the pages of the essay and studied the nicely formatted footnotes at the end, then added the paper to the small pile on the corner of his desk. He was segregating the really good essays, the ones that were well-written and well thought out and researched. The ones that had been written and sold by hungry graduate students, in other words, because no way did any of the knucklehead freshmen in his Intro to American Political History write these small gems.

What to do, what to do. They were originals, that was the problem. He could run a poorly written plagiarism through any number of online databases like Turnitin, catch the lazy sons of bitches that way. But this latest batch of papers was too well done for that. He mentally reviewed the current crop of grad students in his reading seminar on international leadership and political theory. They weren't a bad bunch, but he didn't think any single one of them would quote W.E.B. Du Bois, the Inaugural Address of JFK, and the letters of Lord Byron to reference a single point on how a people lost their free will.

He pushed back from his desk and walked to the window of his office at the University of New Mexico. The grounds were spring green and cool, and the kids were lying about on the grassy knolls, earbuds in place and phones in their hands. He wondered if they were so distracted by their ever-present electronics that any deep thinking, the type of deep thinking that actually led to learning, was impossible. That was the problem, he thought, or, one of the problems, because he could make a list of problems without much effort at all. The kids could call up facts with scary quickness, but could they think about them long enough to understand what those facts meant? Was abstract thinking going the way of the dodo?

Good God. He sounded like an old man. He felt like one too, railing at the failures and posturing of the new generation, kids so young and so clueless, soft as a bunch of newly hatched baby birds, he sometimes wondered if they even had a language in common. It had been a bitch of a year. He looked at the calendar on his wall, another anachronism he wasn't ready to give up, a calendar made out of paper, and onto which a person could write notes—and saw he was two days shy of the one-year mark since he'd retired from the army. Two days past his fifty-second birthday.

The first year out of the military was a tough adjustment for most people, but he'd never really thought it would be a problem for him. He'd been preparing for his retirement career for over five years, doing postdoctoral seminars in political history and educational theory, studying the new technologies that allowed professors to teach online. His field of study was leadership. He'd been as organized and efficient as anyone could be, but he'd not been prepared for the fact he didn't like the little shits he was supposed to be teaching to lead the world for the next fifty years.

It alarmed him, this desire to slap some sense into the kids. His image of himself was mellow, Zen calm in the face of crisis, a deep and original thinker. He'd spent an entire career around young men and women. Maybe the kids who joined the military were different, a little more structured? Considerably more disciplined? Or maybe over the last years of his career, as he'd moved up the ladder, he'd been insulated from the kids by the senior enlisted and his officers. Maybe the majority of the screwups and boneheaded behavior had been dealt with at a lower level, and he'd never even known about it.

If he was being honest, though, he would also have to admit he'd been lonelier than he'd expected to be, now that he was retired. Once you're out, you're out, and he missed the company of the men he'd spent his life with. He had friends, but it wasn't the same as serving together, wearing the same uniform, having a mission in common, and the feeling of yearning for something lost, of missing something vital, had been twisting his stomach for months. He'd gone to see a doctor, even, and been told to take Prilosec. They'd wanted to schedule him for an endoscopy, but he never went back. The Prilosec did nothing, which confirmed his belief that what was sitting in his stomach like a ball of lead was loneliness.

He stared at the small stack of essays on his desk. Enough. What was he going to do about this?

HE WAITED until the majority of the kids had unplugged themselves from their various wires. The seminar was small, and they sat around tables to facilitate lively discussion and debate. The tables also allowed him to walk around behind them and see who was texting on their phones under the edge of the table, but that was just a perk. He handed back the essays. "Really very interesting work by many of you. So interesting, in fact, that I would like to know more about your topics and research. We're going to do an oral defense of your papers, and the final grade will be a combination of both your written work and the oral defense."

A couple of kids were so pale and sick they looked like they were going to throw up. He pointed to Seymour White, the alleged author of the W.E.B. Du Bois masterpiece. "Mr. White, we'll start with you."

THE DEAN of students leaned back in his chair. "John, I have to say I'm impressed. Your documentation is flawless. I wouldn't expect anything less. But just to brief me, how did you manage to fail 89% of your entire freshman class at the final exam?"

"I was expecting it to be worse, but some of them have the makings of world-class bullshit artists," John said.

"You made them give oral defenses of their final essays, is that what I understand?"

"All they had to do was describe the topic of the essay, two major sources, and their conclusions. A single conclusion was all I asked for."

"So am I to understand they not only bought their papers, they didn't even bother to read them before they turned them in? Lazy little shits." The dean grinned at him. "But still, we have a problem."

The general narrowed his eyes at the dean, but otherwise was quite still.

"The complaint was made, and is, I'm afraid, a valid complaint, that the oral defense of the final essay was not described in the syllabus. You can't change your scoring at the last minute and add a new requirement. But," he sat up, a smile brightening his face, "I understand you scared a couple of them so badly they're changing majors from political science to health care. God knows we need more nurses. You're a legend, General. Brass balls and all that. But figure out what to do about your grades, okay? We need them by close of business today."

"SO WHAT did you do?"

John shook his head and reached for the black pepper. "I never assumed they would let me fail the entire class. I had backup grades ready." He twisted the grinder, and the ripe sweet spice of fresh black pepper on a grilled sirloin filled his nose.

"Of course you did."

He looked up at the laughter in Gabriel's voice. Gabriel Sanchez, Chief Warrant Officer-5, retired, his oldest friend. They had served together as comrades and brothers-in-arms on five continents and through every American conflict for more than twenty-five years. They understood each other, because both had followed the warrior's path since they'd been young men. Warriors put honor first, and service, and the safety of the tribe. Everyone called Gabriel the Horse-Lord, for the lethal Apache helicopters he'd flown. "So how are you? What's happening in your house?"

He watched the line deepen between Gabriel's eyebrows as he frowned. "All quiet on the Western front." He hesitated, then, "Juan is having some trouble in school. Flunked algebra and he's trying to pretend he doesn't care. He's acting weird. I don't know what's going on with him."

"He's fourteen, right?"

"Yeah. Though he seems to be swinging wildly between eight and forty. Martha had to put a parental filter on the computers because he was looking at porn. It was cartoon porn, for Christ's sake. I mean that literally—cartoon girls with big startled eyes and cartoon dicks thicker than my fist. Martha is pissed at me because I laughed about it, told her to blow it off. She went off on both of us about disrespecting women."

"You ever look at porn when you were a kid?" John smiled across the table, picturing Gabriel at fourteen.

"I tried to, but all that was available was *National Geographic*, and I just wasn't that interested in breasts. I did jerk off to a picture of an Apache attack helo when I was in high school."

"I believe that. How's Martie? I can't believe she's already eight."

"She's good." Gabriel cut into his steak. "Very bossy and thinks she knows everything. She would have been the one kid in your class who wrote her own paper and leapt at the chance of an oral defense. You'd have had to give her a time limit, otherwise she'd have defended for an hour."

"I had one of those kids. Her paper was only marginally interesting and adequately researched but she was very pleased with herself for actually having written it herself, as opposed to the rest of the class. She was so smug I was afraid one of the other kids might drag her into an alley and punch her in the mouth." John did not ask about Martha, Gabriel's wife. He felt a little constraint about Martha, as if that private part of his friend's life was off-limits to him.

"So where's Kim? I thought I'd see him a bit more since he's staying in your garage."

John shook his head. "Talk about swinging wildly between eight and forty. He's dyed a bright blue streak in his hair. Said something about a person called Perry making 'blue happen,' and now he's got a blue braid hanging down in his face while he eats. School is still too easy for him, so he's not taking it seriously, and he's got a job down at Ho Ho's, cooking Chinese food. I see him working a wok when he should be in class. He's in grad school, the MFA in photography."

"Ho Ho's? You mean that place on the corner of Yale and Central?"

John nodded. "He claims it's the favorite restaurant of the homeless in Albuquerque."

Gabriel studied him, then ate a forkful of baked potato. "Actually, I didn't know homeless people had a favorite restaurant."

"That's what I said, too, and got a lecture about park benches not being equipped with microwaves, and what were they supposed to do? Apparently, Ho Ho's is cheap and gives large portions with lots of rice and noodles, so they can share with each other. This makes the restaurant popular with both the homeless and the hungry student population. But he might have just been winding me up."

"Kim's Korean. That place is Chinese."

"He claims all chinks are welcome at Ho Ho's. It's actually owned by a couple of Vietnamese sisters."

John pushed his empty plate away. "You want to have coffee at my place?"

He felt Gabriel watching him, but he kept his eyes on the table. Then he looked at his old friend, felt the warmth, and the welcome, in dark eyes brown as sandalwood.

Gabriel was smiling at him. "Yeah, I would. It's been a while. Too long if you ask me."

Just what John was thinking.

Gabriel followed him home from the restaurant, parked his pickup truck behind John's car in the driveway. Inside, John pulled out the Kona Gold coffee beans from the cabinet and put a handful in the grinder, listened while Gabriel settled into the couch. He stretched his arms out along the top of the couch, laid his head back and sighed. His eyes were closed, his face relaxed. Not many people got to see Gabriel like this.

When the coffee finished brewing, John carried a couple of mugs into the living room and handed one to Gabriel. He set his cup down on the coffee table and settled down next to him on the couch. "So what's been happening with you? You've been in practice about six months. Is the law what you were hoping it would be?"

Gabriel had his nose in the cup, smelling the rich coffee. "Yeah, it's good. Fine. Not...."

Not like the army. He didn't need to say it. John felt it too. "You miss it still?" Gabriel nodded. "Yeah, me too. But it's a young man's game."

Gabriel had finished law school the year before, deciding on a midlife career in public service. John also suspected he was doing it to make Martha happy. She'd been a good army wife, following him across the world, managing the family while he was deployed. John thought she would like being a lawyer's wife. "I don't like the young lawyers right out of school much. I sound like an old man, looking at them and thinking what a bunch of selfish, spoiled little pricks they are. Money, money, money. You could take the whole crowd of them right off a cliff following the sweet green scent of money. I don't know, John. I look at them and think, who the fuck is left? Where are the leaders? Is there an ounce of fortitude in any of them? They get hysterical when they can't remember the pocket where they stowed their phones."

John picked up his cup and drank the coffee down. "Now you know why I had a shit fit and pretended to flunk my entire freshman class. Not that I think it did any good. I just wanted to see if any single one of them would stand up and admit they hadn't a clue because they'd bought their papers."

"Did they?"

John shook his head.

14

"I like the practice, though. It's like the law firm of last resort. For the clueless and the desperate. And the broke. I don't think I'll ever have a pot to piss in. But I'm always happy to stick a thorn in the fat asses of the establishment." Gabriel reached out and took his empty cup. "You want a refill?"

"No. I think I'm going to grab a quick shower. Finish what's in the pot if you want."

John stepped into the shower off his bedroom, gave himself a brisk scrub-down. He toweled off and wrapped the towel around his waist. Gabriel was waiting for him, sitting on the side of the bed. He'd undressed down to his boxers, clothes neatly folded over the back of a chair. He stood and reached out, pulled John closer by the towel around his waist. He leaned forward, moved his warm mouth across John's shoulder, up his neck. "I love the smell of Dial soap on your skin." He pulled the towel away and gathered John into his arms. "My old friend. I can't tell you how much I've missed you."

"Hello, Gabriel." John reached up, traced his fingers along Gabriel's strong jawline, across a mouth that had always curved into a smile at his touch. Gabriel moved his hand down into the curly brown hair that covered John's belly and chest, still mostly brown, with just a few notes of silver. Gabriel said the silver looked good, matched the color of his eyes.

CHAPTER 2

GABRIEL STAYED longer than usual, drowsing against John's shoulder, touching his skin. When he'd left, late enough he'd have to come up with a good excuse for Martha, he'd pressed John's palm to his mouth, his eyes closed, like he was imprinting the feel of John's skin in his memory. John did that too. He thought sometimes his secret life gave him a strength he wouldn't have had otherwise. His memories, his time with Gabriel, seemed colored like autumn leaves, a quiet, golden joy that sat near his heart and sustained his spirit.

He was thinking about something Gabriel had said, about how hard it was to find anything real in the world. John had felt this too. Was it the changing times or the changes in them as they got older? The warrior's life was simple, basic, but very real. Reality focused your mind until it was as sharp as a spear. But when old warriors retired, their armor started falling away, and the noise of the world crowded in.

The door from the garage flew open, and Kim danced into the kitchen, waving something that looked like pieces of a science experiment. Kim never just walked into a room. Since he was a toddler, he'd burst or danced or flew. The art of a dramatic entrance was in his back pocket. "How's my favorite uncle this morning? I would have brought this over last night but I saw you had the Horse-Lord in for some evening coffee. He stayed late, huh? You confirmed bachelors must have had a lot to talk about?"

"He's not a confirmed bachelor, Kim. He's married and has a family." John felt a little irritated at his darling nephew. "Don't be an ass. We've been friends since Beirut."

That got him a flash of disapproving black eyes. Kim unloaded his armful of glass beakers onto the cabinet and started assembling them. "What is it with you military guys? You don't talk in years. You talk in events, like you were there. *We've been friends since Beirut.* Oh! Wait a minute! You *were* in Beirut!"

John didn't need to say anything. Kim would act whether he had an audience or not, like his life was one long comic monologue.

"Ta da! How do you like this? Isn't it a beauty? Where's that Kona coffee?"

What was that thing? It was a collection of glass beakers and bulbous jars hooked together by spirals of glass pipette. "Kim, have you made an illegal still? Please don't blow up the garage."

"It's not a still! But you're very close. It's a coffee pot. But that's like saying the space shuttle is just a big airplane. This baby brings a whole new level of science to the art of coffee brewing."

"Does the art of coffee brewing need new science? I thought you said the French press was the pinnacle…. Never mind. Okay, so how does this work?"

Kim was filling the top glass bulb with water filtered through the Brita pitcher. He fitted a black rubber stopper in the bottom and attached a length of glass pipette to a hole in the rubber. He poured coffee grounds into another glass ball and fitted the pieces back together. "This baby is worth grinding fresh beans."

They both stared at the coffee machine. John thought he noticed a structural problem. "Kim, I don't see how the water will ever come in contact with the coffee." The two elements were separated by several lengths of curly glass tubing.

"Oh, it does! Just one drop at a time."

"One drop at a time," John repeated. "And so this one drop falls into the coffee? One drop at a time? So how long does it take to brew a… bulbful? And how does it stay hot until you drink it?"

"See, it's not designed for a quick morning cuppa. It's an all-day-long affair, this coffee. And you don't drink it hot. You drink it cold." Kim was giving him a look now, daring him to say anything. John had long experience with this nephew, though, and his projects, so he moved to the French press and poured himself a cup.

Kim studied his contraption and John studied him. He was dressed in a black tee shirt that said Ho Ho's on the front, decorated with a graphic that appeared to be a huge, yawning mouth, with teeth and tongue, and a pair of old camo pants that had belonged to John back when they were still wearing camo for the jungle, not the desert. "Are you going to work? You don't have any classes?"

"I've got a class at eleven. I'm going in to do the lunch prep. I've got to work tonight, though, so don't wait up for me."

John stared at the back of his head until Kim whirled around, setting the pale blue braid near his left eye whirling. "What?"

John had been thinking about the group of reference books on his desk and a nephew who was too smart for his own good. A nephew with a peculiar sense of humor. "Read anything by W.E.B. Du Bois lately?"

Kim widened his eyes, a look of such innocence John knew he had him. "What in the hell were you thinking? I nearly flunked the entire class. I made them do an oral defense of their papers. I should have known. You're the only person who knew I had just reread *The Souls of Black Folks*."

Now Kim was genuinely shocked. "An oral defense? Are you kidding me? Holy shit! But why the whole class? I only wrote five of them. You're pretty slow on the uptake, Uncle John. I thought you would have figured it out by the first paper."

"I estimate one out of twelve students actually wrote their own paper." He sat down at the table. Kim did not look the least guilty or sorry. He looked like he had pulled off a huge prank. "Kim, can you please just…." He didn't know what to say. So what was new? Kim had been rendering him speechless for years.

Kim swooped down and landed a kiss on his forehead. "Not to worry, Uncle dear. I have a career plan, I promise I do. I made two hundred and seventy-five bucks off the papers, but that's just chump change, and it gave me a chance to stretch my brain. I've got bigger plans. I'm going to be a drag queen!"

KIM HAD been the darling of his tiny Catholic orphanage in Seoul. There was no question, from the moment he had crawled delightedly into John's sister's arms, which baby they were going to take home. John's sister and her husband had stayed with him on base while they worked through the lengthy system for foreign adoption. The Koreans required a six-month wait between the initial application, done in person, and the final award of adoption. When they had gone back to the States for their six-month wait, John had walked the two miles from his quarters to the orphanage nearly every evening to check on Kim. Kim would see him from across the tiny playroom and climb over the furniture and any playmates in his way to get to his big uncle. The boy would reach his leg, and then tug on the cuff of his pants. Two tugs, and John would reach down and pick him up. It was their secret signal. Kim still did it, though John couldn't believe he remembered that far back. When he was in trouble, when he'd been so outrageous he scared himself, he would curl up next to John and give his sleeve a couple of tugs. And John knew it meant his baby needed to be picked up, lifted high above the scary world.

IT HAD been a long and dull week, and John was happy to hear Gabriel's voice. "I'd like to see General Mitchel if he's available."

John listened from his office. His shared admin, Cynthia, had been in a snit for two days. "We have a *Dr.* Mitchel here. Is that who you mean?"

Gabriel didn't say anything. A firm, upright posture, calm face, and silence, left most of the world rethinking what they'd just said, and scrambling to readjust.

"Just wait a minute. I'll see if he's free."

"No need, thank you, Cynthia." John was at the door, held out his hand to Gabriel.

"Sir, do you have a few minutes?"

"Yes, of course. Come on in." John looked at Cynthia, didn't say anything until she broke eye contact and started searching her desktop. "Will you hold my calls, please?"

"Yes, of course, General. I mean, Dr. Mitchel." Her face was shading to red now. She was the kind of woman who seemed to attract little cloudbursts of drama and disaster. John did not give her the attention her behavior usually garnered from older male faculty members, and he was wondering what she would do next to punish him.

John closed the door. "Hi, Gabriel. You got time for coffee?"

"Sure."

"This pot of coffee took over twelve hours to brew. Kim's rigged up some contraption that's taken over the kitchen. I set it up at night and pour two smallish cups into a thermos in the morning. He instructed me to drink it cold but I believe in the power of microwaves."

"That's one of those cold coffee brewers?" John looked at him in surprise. "I've seen one. Martha showed me in the store. Seems to me if you want cold coffee, you can brew a pot in five minutes and then let it sit around until it gets cold."

"Or you can dump some coffee grounds in a pot and pour in the water and let it sit until you've got thirty seconds to drink it. I've had coffee like that lots of times. With you, if I recall correctly."

"It was pretty damn good at the time."

"So, did Martha buy one?"

Gabriel shook his head. "I said something like 'the Emperor has no goddamn clothes on,' and she got embarrassed and called me an asshole and left me in the store."

John poured two cups and put them in the microwave to heat. "Family okay?"

Gabriel shrugged and sat down in one of the chairs facing John's desk. "Families are really hard work some days. No, not some days, most days." He turned to John, ran both hands back through his dark hair. "You remember when we were in Bahrain? And we went downtown and ate at that place that had the good tandoori?"

"The place with the donkey walking in a circle next to the well?"

"Yes, exactly. I think that donkey walked in circles for his entire life, around and around and around, pumping the water. That was his life. If he slowed down, the old man hit him with a switch. They let him loose when he dropped dead. Today I feel like that donkey." He was speaking very carefully. Men like them, they gave up a lot to have families. Peace of mind, mostly. Free time. All of their money. "We should have kicked that old man down the well and busted the donkey loose. He wouldn't have made it very many days, running wild in the souk, but he would have died free."

"You're such an American."

Gabriel looked good. He was wearing a pair of charcoal-gray trousers with a nice military crease and a pale blue button-down. His tie was an elegant red with pale blue stripes. John enjoyed looking at a well-groomed man, one who took pride in himself and his appearance. He handed Gabriel a cup when the bell rang on the microwave. His skin was the warm brown of coffee with lots of cream. Not that either of them indulged in cream, not at their age. John took the other chair facing his desk and set his coffee down. "How do you like it?"

"Tastes good. Fancy," he added. "Rich berry notes, as Kim would say. You can count on the kids to take something utterly simple and make it more complicated than it needs to be. I think they're bored. Did you see that kid cooking empanadas with a solar oven down on Central?" John nodded. "I tasted one. Pretty good."

"First time I saw his truck, I thought he was trying to contact aliens with that thing. Send a beacon into space. And it didn't strike me as the least bit odd he would be doing that in front of the university."

Gabriel set his coffee cup down on the edge of the desk. "Have you seen Kim the last couple of days?"

"No. I've heard him come in from work but he's usually still asleep when I leave in the morning."

"I went into Ho Ho's at lunch today." He shook his head slowly. "That is the most dysfunctional excuse for a restaurant I have ever seen. I saw two women get into a food fight, screaming and throwing pot stickers at each other's heads. After it was all over, they got out a push broom and swept everything up."

"Two students?"

"No! Two of the women behind the counter! The ones serving food!"

John was laughing now. "Oh, God. That sort of place would hold a magnetic attraction for Kim." He studied Gabriel's face, saw some lingering trouble. "What's wrong?"

"Somebody took a punch at his pretty face. He's got a fat lip and what looks like a little mouse under his right eye." He held up a hand, and John realized he'd stood, pushed his chair back. "Hold on, partner. Let's think for a minute. Don't go in without backup."

John sat back down, felt his face shading dark with embarrassment. "Did you have a trial today? You're looking very lawyerly."

Gabriel nodded. "Mock trial at the law school. One of my old profs asked me to help out. The rest of the crew struck a blow for freedom of expression and wore hoodies. I blew them out of the water before the game started by reminding them of their grandfathers. They were distracted and off their game from the moment I walked in the room."

John suspected the girl lawyers and probably some of the boys had not been thinking about their grandfathers when they studied Gabriel in dress clothes. "You look good."

They looked at each other then, really looked, the way they did in private, and John felt something warm and welcoming in Gabriel's brown eyes. Gabriel stood, put his hand on John's cheek, left it there for one intimate moment. "It's nearly two. The lunch crowd is clearing out. I'll go with you, rearguard action only. He'll tell you what happened. I'll just sit there and keep him from bolting for the door."

22

KIM WENT for bold when he saw the two of them walk in, his eyes as blank and glassy as obsidian, though the fat lip gave him a bit of a lisp. "Hello, Uncle. Would you like some lunch? I could make you a good stir-fry, or a bowl of soup if you want something light."

"I'm not here for something to eat."

"Really? That's unfortunate, since this is a restaurant and I'm the cook and currently on duty. I can't leave my post to chat with my favorite uncle and the Horse-Lord." Gabriel had been riding Kim around on his shoulders, his big horsey, since Seoul.

"Okay. Then I'll have a pot of tea and a bowl of soup for two."

Kim narrowed his eyes at Gabriel, sitting at the table by the door, his long legs crossed and checking messages on his phone. "I knew he would squeal. Four eighty-five."

"That's a good price for tea and soup," John said, handing over a five-dollar bill. "You can keep the change as a tip for your excellent service."

Kim carefully placed the fifteen cents in the glass jar on the counter with the paper sign taped to the side that said TIPS. The sign was worn, the tape peeling off from the dog-eared edges. "Thank you so much!" The change tinkled when it hit the bottom of the empty jar.

The restaurant looked worn, with dull linoleum floors and the sort of tables and plastic chairs that were sitting in low-rent diners all over America. The air smelled like tired oil and soy sauce and green onions, and the large, glass front windows were smudged. Two elderly Oriental women, with identical helmets of graying hair, had their arms around each other behind the serving line. They were leaning their heads together. John looked over at Gabriel. Surely these weren't the two in the pot-sticker fight? Gabriel nodded. Oh, yes, they were.

John joined him at the table by the door. "We're having soup and tea." He looked back at the kitchen, the cook stations visible over the top of the glass serving line. Kim kept his back to them, busy with his knife and a cutting board. "He's going to pretend nothing happened. Look at him. He's trying to come up with a decent excuse right now."

KIM SET bowls of soup on the table, then poured two thimble-size celadon cups of jasmine tea. John wondered where he had unearthed the good china. The soup was creamy, fragrant with a coconut broth, and had in the middle of the bowl a little pile of green onions and tiny pieces of carrot sliced into miniature flowers. Gabriel took a spoonful. "This is really good, Kim. Did you make this?"

"No, we have some Chinese elves back in the kitchen. I just crack the whip and keep them working." He turned to John and flipped the blue braid over his shoulder. "Nothing happened. It was an accident, a fluke. I swear."

John picked up his cup and took a sip of tea, but he kept his eyes on Kim. Gabriel put his spoon down and picked up his cup, studied Kim like he was a little bird that had just flown into the wrong nest. Kim crossed his arms and looked from one to the other. "The silent treatment doesn't work on me anymore. I'm not twelve, in case you've forgotten."

John put down the teacup and picked up his spoon. Gabriel was right. The soup was good, very good, delicate and light, with a subtle green flavor and a hint of woody mushroom underneath.

"What do you think? Good, right?"

The black eye was a little puffy and bruised, looked about two days old. The lip was swollen with a tiny cut. Those types of cuts usually came from a person's teeth when they were slapped or hit in the mouth. Not together, though. It looked like two separate blows. He looked down at Kim's right hand. The knuckles were smooth, no sign of redness or abrasion. Whatever had happened, he hadn't hit back.

Gabriel picked up the little teapot and refilled both of their cups.

"All right! Fine! I told you about it, Uncle John, remember? I didn't think you believed me. Per usual." John took another spoonful of soup. It was outstanding. Who knew Kim could cook like this? "Okay, it was another drag queen."

"*Another* drag queen?"

"Okay, so I'm not exactly a drag queen yet, but I told you, remember? It's just performance art, you know? Performance art that speaks to who I am as a gay man. Speaks *honestly*. *Truthfully*. Something the two of you ought to consider, before you start casting stones. At least people my age don't hide the fact they're gay. We're living with it right out in the open, black eyes and all. Whatever the consequences. *Not* in hiding. "

John and Gabriel exchanged a look, and John put down his napkin and rose. "Performance art. I see. So, if I want to get slapped around by a drag queen, I will certainly take your advice and engage in some performance art. Thank you for the soup. I'll speak to you at home."

Gabriel was standing next to the table, staring at Kim, his hands on his hips. Kim reached over and gave him a quick hug around the waist. "I know, I know, I'm such a bitch, right? I don't know what's wrong with me. Just ignore me when I get like this, okay?"

Gabriel gave the blue braid a sharp tug. "Don't worry, brat. I always do."

JOHN WAS steaming. It was unusual for him, because he was a man who favored action over reaction. And like most military men, he thought there was nearly always a peaceful solution if people used their brains first, before their mouths. Well, maybe 98 percent of the time there was a peaceful solution. Maybe in some parts of the world, that number would have to drop to well below 75 percent. But at his kitchen table, in Albuquerque, New Mexico?

Kim had put a toe across an unspoken barrier, one that had never before been breached. He waited until Kim came home, at a reasonable hour for once. Kim came into the kitchen and sat down at the table like he'd come to play a game of cards. John gave him a cool look out of cool gray eyes. "What do you think you're doing?" His voice was very soft, the dangerous one that his officers and men understood meant trouble.

At least Kim didn't pretend not to understand. "You're not in the army any longer. 'Don't Ask, Don't Tell' has been repealed, remember? I should ask you what you think *you're* doing."

"What does that have to do with such an egregious breach of my privacy in a public place? But we're not going to talk about me, because this isn't about me, right? Why would you try to hurt Gabriel that way? You know he's got a family, kids. His son is fourteen. Whatever private life he's chosen, it's his private life, do you understand? His privacy. His life. You don't own it, you don't have any piece in it, and you don't get to decide about the flow of information. How dare you, Kim?" Kim stared down at the table, eyes glistening. "But I don't think you were trying to hurt him. You knew it would hurt me. Weak fighters always go for a sucker punch on their way to the floor."

Tears were standing in Kim's eyes, and he looked as furious as John felt. "Of course it would hurt you! Because you've loved him for years. He's been your lover for years. You think I don't know? It just pisses me off that you're living some kind of half-life, and dragging him into the shadows with you, just to, what, protect your reputation? I mean, I don't get it. You're retired now. It's been a year. I thought you would step up and claim your life! You put it on hold for the military, I get it. There is a price to pay to serve, I understand that. You explained it to me and I accepted it. It was important work and somebody had to do it. But do you really think what you have is the best there is, or even in any way an acceptable life? If I had really thought, right about the time I realized I was gay, that the sort of life you lived was what my life was destined to be, I would have swallowed a handful of pills and been done with it."

John gripped the edge of the tabletop. "And do you really think life as a gay man was the same in 1972 as 2012? You think those years didn't matter? You don't know dick about my life, and you're making a mistake if you're trying to outthink me. I am not what this is about. Now, you tell me right now what the fuck happened to your face, or you can go out to the garage and start packing."

Kim stared down at the wooden tabletop for a long time, and then he reached across and took John's wrist between two fingers. John let go of the tabletop and Kim slid his hand into his. "I'm sorry. And I'll tell the Horse-Lord I'm sorry too. I was out of line."

"What happened?"

"I went out with this guy I met. It was okay at first. Then he started getting physical. You know, just a little too rough when he grabbed my arm. Maybe he'd try to hold me in my seat when I wanted to get up. I caught him checking the numbers on my phone a few nights ago, and he made some joke about watching what I was doing. Keeping an eye on me. It just... I don't know. He was making me nervous. Sending up red flags. I knew something wasn't right. So I told him I wanted to take it easy, back off a little bit, see other people. He backhanded me. That's when my lip got cut. Then he looked at me and very deliberately hit me again. I think he wanted to mark me, you know? Put his mark on my face."

"Is he a student here?"

Kim shook his head. "No, not a student. Uncle John, you've got to promise me you won't go off."

"Why would I go off?"

"He's one of my instructors."

JOHN EXTRACTED the necessary information, and then he kissed his baby on the forehead and made grilled cheese and chicken noodle soup for supper. They played Crazy Eights until Kim got quiet again, and he took his phone and went off to the garage to call Gabriel. John didn't think Kim had seen Gabriel flinch in the restaurant. He'd covered it quickly enough, but John had seen it, seen the way Gabriel's jaw tightened, like he was getting ready for a blow.

But do you really think what you have is the best there is, or even in any way an acceptable life? Kim's words felt like a dirge in his head. What John thought was he was doing the best that anyone could, given a similar set of circumstances. But was that really good enough? Was he dragging Gabriel into some sort of shadow life, not fully here or there? No, he wasn't. Gabriel didn't get dragged anywhere. They'd both made their choices a long time ago, and he thought Gabriel, just like himself, was happy for the grace notes in his life, the few hours they could be themselves, with all their public masks removed, a few gentle and intimate hours between friends. Wasn't that the best one could ask for? A life of service to others, with the occasional grace note? So why did he still feel so lonely? Why had so much of this last year been spent feeling an ache for something he couldn't describe even to himself?

Gabriel had been a Horse-Lord long before Kim started calling him by that name. He'd been a squadron leader when he was a young pilot, always had the most fearless flyers in his group. Gabriel's squadrons were named after the famous horse warriors of the past, and he'd ridden his Apache like it was a wild pony, just barely under his control. When John flew with him the first time, his group was named for the horse warriors of the plains, the Sioux, and Gabriel's chopper was named in honor of Crazy Horse. When they made love for the first time, Gabriel had been channeling the great Mongol warlord, Genghis Khan.

CHAPTER 3

JOHN SUSPECTED he wouldn't hear from Gabriel for a while, after Kim's drama-queen performance at Ho Ho's. He had his family and his new law practice, after all, and neither one left a lot of free time for dinner with old friends and their pain-in-the-ass nephews. So he was pleasantly surprised when Gabriel sent him an email, inviting him to go to the ball game on Friday night with himself and his son, Juan. John was a fan of the Albuquerque Isotopes, the local minor league team. They worked hard and had occasional victories which made everyone in town feel a little more hopeful about the state of the world.

It had been more than six months since he had seen Juan, so he didn't know about the shaggy hair. When he was younger, Juan had sported hair like his father's, a trim military cut. Now he looked like one of the Beatles, about 1965, and he reached up every few seconds and pressed his bangs down over his forehead, like he was trying to get the hair to grow faster. He had braces too, something new. John wasn't sure which of these changes to mention, given the drooping shoulders, sullen face, and general look of misery. Juan was acting like he was being dragged to the brig, not to the ball game. They found their seats, just left of home plate, and Gabriel gave Juan twenty dollars. "This is for food. Don't make yourself sick." He handed over two additional twenties. "This is for either a cap or a tee shirt. If you can't wear it to school, it's not okay with me or your mother. And I want the change and a receipt."

Juan pocketed the cash with a nod, then escaped to the food court. John turned to watch him climb the stairs. The food court at Isotopes Park was a madhouse of American gluttony. You could get a foot-long Coney or Chicago dog, of course, but also pizza, pork tamales, shrimp stir-fry, funnel cakes with powdered sugar on top, and vindaloo curry. The flavors of these competing cuisines mixed with the smell of spilled beer and popcorn that hung like a cloud over the park. "Is he okay up there by himself?"

Gabriel nodded. "Apparently he's meeting some of his crew from school, which is the only reason he agreed to come."

"I remember when he used to walk behind you and try to match his stride with yours. He'd have to take a couple of running steps to catch you up every few seconds. Then he'd try to match your steps again."

"Those days are long gone." Gabriel looked out over the park. "Now I'm unbearably stupid and too embarrassing to be seen with in public." The groundskeepers were finishing the white lines, and a group of kids dressed in food costumes, a burger and a hotdog and a taco, were having a footrace out behind second base. Four middle-aged women in matching purple tee shirts were preparing to sing, standing next to a microphone, and a retired astronaut was pitching a ball to the catcher, getting ready to throw out the first ball of the game. The setting sun touched Gabriel's face, turned his skin gold, and John looked at the laugh lines that fanned out from his eyes.

Gabriel turned in his seat, looked at John with a smile in his eyes. "What are you looking at?" His eyes were the dark brown of very old Irish whiskey, and John smelled cedar and orange in his aftershave.

John turned back to the park, watched the big orange mascot, Astro, shake his butt at the little taco, winner of the footrace. "Just admiring the fine view." He could feel Gabriel smiling next to him. "You want a beer? I'll drive if you need something stronger."

"They don't make anything strong enough for the father of a fourteen-year-old son. A son who has decided he wants to go to college to be a video game tester. I told Martha I'd pay for the braces but I wasn't going to pay for college to teach him how to play video games.

She said we have to support him and let him make his own choices. Really? I don't think so, not at fourteen. He's like one of those soft-shell crabs in the middle of molting. Not ready to make choices about anything. Absolutely at risk from any passing predator. Dumb as a fucking stone. That's why he's not speaking to me. I told him he can't be a video game tester, and then he says why don't I know he hates seafood?"

"You shared with him the soft-shell crab analogy?"

Gabriel nodded. "That was probably a mistake."

"It's early days yet. I think Kim was fourteen when he wanted to be an ice skater."

Gabriel turned in his seat and grinned. "Yeah, well, it's all just performance art with that kid, isn't it? I think I will take that beer. Tell them to float a piece of lime in the neck."

When John got back with a couple of beers, Juan was showing his father his new tee shirt. Gabriel was holding it up, and the look on his face was one John had seen before. The shirt was black, a size 2XL, and the picture showed a babe in Daisy Dukes, breasts popping out of the cut in her torn tee shirt, straddling a big bike, holding a beer in each hand. Coronas. John stared down at the beers he was carrying. Coronas, one in each hand. "Good God."

Gabriel shoved the tee shirt back at Juan, who put it in the bag. He showed a grin full of braces. "So, I can tell Mom you're okay with it?"

"Take it back and exchange it for something else. Like, right now." Gabriel stared at Juan the entire way down the aisle before he turned back to John. "That little wiseass."

John handed over his beer. "The look on your face reminded me of that time, where were we, Ivory Coast? You remember? You caught that mechanic sitting on his ass, puffing on a cigar and talking to his girl back home when he was supposed to be doing maintenance on your chopper."

"I might not have kicked his ass so hard but he was smoking that piece of shit cigar in my hanger." He looked over at John, took a long pull on his beer. "Okay, well, I would have kicked his ass regardless. He was begging for it. Seems like just yesterday, but that was '90, right? '91?"

"Must have been '89. We were in the Middle East in '90. Well, time goes by."

"You got that right, brother." They clicked their beer bottles together, a quiet salute to the times. "So, what did Kim have to say? He wouldn't tell me anything on the phone. Said you had the details. He was very charming in his apology, by the way. I assume you chewed him a new one?"

"That I did. He has been dating an abusive professor."

"What, you mean one of his grad school profs? He's doing an MFA in the arts, right?"

"Last time I checked it was photography. I talked to the department head, who did not seem surprised—either about the allegations of dating a student or the allegations of abusive behavior. I got the feeling that, as both student and instructor are gay men, this was somehow swept under the rug in a way it would not have been if the student had been a young woman. Like the rules are different based on gender. Is it still so embarrassing to be gay in New Mexico? I wouldn't have thought so. It was ridiculous, the man seemed unable to think in any manner that would lead to a decision! I can't imagine how he runs a committee meeting, much less a graduate department at the university level. So I went to the dean of students and the vice president, let them both know if this matter wasn't handled to my satisfaction within two weeks, I would take further action. The dean actually asked me what further action I had in mind."

"Oh, man, that was a piss-poor move."

"You would think a basic understanding of the nature of strategy and tactics would be required study for any leader in this day and age, much less the leaders of an institution of higher learning, but apparently not. Linear thinking gets a bad rap for not being creative, but at some point decisions need to be made. Conclusions drawn. The entire world can't stop work to brainstorm with their dicks in their hands, fun as that might be."

Gabriel toyed with his bottle, shoved the tiny wedge of lime down into the neck of the beer. "Maybe a deposition, so you can go to the police without having to drag Kim along."

"Who needs to do a deposition? Does it have to be a lawyer?"

32

"I can take the deposition. We really need photos, but I can't see Kim announcing to the world he's a victim. A lawsuit might be worth considering, or just the threat of a lawsuit. We might use the media, as well. Nasty story, that."

They fell silent, listening to the ladies in the purple shirts sing an old-fashioned barbershop song, "Down by the Old Mill Stream," then John Fogerty took over the loudspeakers, singing *put me in, Coach, I'm ready to play.*

Gabriel drained the bottle of beer and put the empty in the seat holder. "One of his professors. What in the hell is wrong with people, they think they can do anything and get away with it? Everyone seems to understand the nature of free choice but no one understands consequences."

John stared out across the field, watched the ball players line up, their caps over their hearts. "I am going to make sure this little prick understands clearly the consequences before he touches another young man."

"DEAN FOX! We don't see you in this building nearly often enough!" John could tell Cynthia was beaming.

"Cynthia, you are like a ray of sunshine this morning. Do you suppose I could speak to the general for a moment?"

"Yes, of course! I'll just see if he's available."

John stayed behind his desk when Cynthia brought Dean Fox in, but rose to offer a silent handshake.

"So, John, how is your graduate seminar? Theory of Political Leadership, isn't it?"

"Something like that. What can I do for you?"

The dean leaned back in his chair, folded his hands over his belly. "I wonder if you've had a chance to rethink your position vis-à-vis this unfortunate...."

"The episode of physical assault by a professor toward a student? Rethink in what way, Dean?"

"When we spoke last, I recommended you consider the political realities of this situation. That's your field, after all. I mean, no one understands politics the way you do without understanding the art of the compromise."

"Actually, I'm here to teach leadership theory. Leadership, not politics. Unfortunately, they no longer appear to be quite the same thing." John leaned forward, his arms on his desk. "But you're correct. That was your suggestion, and I have done some thinking. I think we will involve the criminal justice system at this point and let them do a proper investigation."

"Now, John, that way, it's never easy on the victims, is it?"

"As opposed to... what? The option would be not becoming victims in the first place?"

"John, the challenge for me is that this particular instructor is the son of a member of the board of supervisors for the university system here in New Mexico. Very powerful man, old school, you know? Long years of developing relationships, especially among the senior leadership at this university. He never forgets an enemy, and he keeps a tight hold of the fiscal reins."

"Ah. I see." John sat back, studied the other man. "And do you suppose this old-school man knows what his son is doing in Albuquerque?"

The dean studied the view out John's window. "Nice office, this. They say the apple doesn't fall far from the tree. That's what I've heard, anyway."

"You could say that about my nephew as well. He's much more like me than anyone realizes." The alarm on the dean's face at this statement was all John could have wished.

JOHN HAD no intention of calling the police. He couldn't without Kim's consent, and if he was sure of anything, it was that Kim did not want the police involved. But the threat was a decent diversion, and it also made a reasonable backup plan.

"One could say that self-portraiture is a form of meditation." Kim slid a piece of toast and egg onto John's plate. "There you go. Toad in a Hole."

"Self-portraits are a form of meditation? Maybe a form of psychotherapy. I would hesitate to suggest self-indulgence." The egg was fried into a missing round of the toast, the whole slathered with butter. A grilled tomato joined the Toad on his plate.

"Maybe meditation is too strong a word. I guess what I mean is photography can be used to learn about yourself. I just think that all the creative arts have a great potential for healing. And people really should be stepping up to the plate and trying to heal themselves." Kim took a bite of his Toad in the Hole. "Hey, that's good. Speaking of stepping up to the plate, how was the ball game?"

"Decent. Not their best effort, and they seemed to be tired by the seventh. They've been on the road for a week. Also, Juan was along and he made it his business to torture his father."

"Oh, I wish I could have seen that! The Horse-Lord brought to his knees!"

John gave him a sharp look. "Not to his knees. Let's call it a draw. But it certainly appeared to exhaust them both."

"What is he, twelve?"

"Fourteen."

"Well, no wonder, then. Hormones are raging! All you want to do when you're fourteen is snatch up a broadsword and hack something to pieces, then find a big rock and fuck it to death."

"Good God." John finished his Toad and pushed his plate back. Kim had made them beans on toast yesterday. Was he about to enter a British phase? John didn't think he could take it if Kim started speaking with a British accent. He picked up the photograph Kim had brought to the table. He'd printed a double self-portrait, the camera covering his left eye and then his right. In one picture, the black eye and busted lip were plainly visible, and in the other, it was covered with his camera.

"You see the difference?"

"Tell me," John said.

35

"Look at the expression in the eyes. You see how I'm looking at myself, when I can see the damage? When it's visible to the world? I look like a cringing dog, afraid to get hit. But the other one, where the damage is hidden, my eyes look different. Stronger. Maybe cooler. My filters are intact."

"What filters?"

"Everyone looks at the world through filters, Uncle John. Usually identity, but it could be culture too, or language or some other form of self-identification. I usually have a gay filter up, and always an artist filter, and a 'being your nephew' filter, that one's in my bones."

John studied the photo. He couldn't see much of a difference in the look in Kim's eyes between the two pictures, but maybe that was because he felt his hands knot into fists and his heart start to pound in his throat when he saw the marks on Kim's face. All he could think of was snatching up a broadsword and hacking something to pieces.

"Okay, so what's your plan?" he asked. "You're going to do a series of self-portraits, showing the abuse on your face, and submit that portfolio to the asshole professor who did the damage?"

Kim was shaking his head. "That would be a subtle punishment for a subtle man, but he's an ape. He'd probably enjoy looking at them. No, I'm not thinking about him. He's out of my head. I'm just keeping the colors bright in my own soul."

Kim smiled at him from across the table, and John remembered a summer's day in the park when Kim was four or five. He'd come whirling across the green grass, his arms outstretched like wings, and he'd announced his soul looked like a butterfly and was full of beautiful colors.

"You know for sure he's done it before?"

Kim nodded. "But don't ask me to break a confidence, Uncle John."

"Of course not. You remember Gabriel's meeting you after lunch today?"

"At Ho Ho's, right? Is he bringing Juan?"

"Not that I know."

"Maybe I'll call him and see if he can come. I'll put him to work bussing tables. Or he can put some pot stickers together." John watched him, a question on his face. "All you want when you're fourteen is to have the opportunity to not be a fool in front of your dad," Kim said.

"And that thing with the big rock."

"Yes, that thing with the big rock."

CHAPTER 4

JOHN DECIDED to drop in and see how the deposition was coming. Even the strongest men sometimes needed backup. Gabriel was a kick-ass chopper pilot. He'd flown into the middle of hornets' nests without blinking in Somalia, Kuwait, Sudan, Haiti, Afghanistan. John had seen him drop quiet as smoke into an LZ the size of a dishtowel to pick up a medevac, drop off water and ammunition to troops under fire. When Gabriel was in the zone, he was a rock. But even a rock could be worn down by the relentless drip-drip-drip of water that was quality time with the kids.

Ho Ho's was late-afternoon quiet. A table near the women's rest room held a young girl, crying silently, wiping her nose on her sleeve, typing into her phone, then crying again. Juan was wearing a black apron with *Ho Ho's* on the front, along with their signature logo of an open, hungry mouth. He was wiping down tables and keeping an alarmed eye on the crying girl. Another table along the back wall held the remains of a lunch special. The man sitting there had put his head back against the wall and closed his eyes, one hand holding the Styrofoam container with his food so no one could take it away. He looked unbearably weary.

Kim was sitting with Gabriel, pouring tea like he was entertaining at Buckingham Palace. Gabriel looked like he was drawing on reserves of patience, but his shirt was still crisp white, and he wore it with a red-and-gray tie and charcoal-gray suit pants. John felt a thump in his gut, a little twist of lust, seeing him looking so fine, face smoothly shaven, eyes dark and as deep as the night sky. Gabriel looked a question at him, because John usually guarded the way he looked at Gabriel in public. Sometimes it was just more than he could do, though, wearing his mask, his professional face, cool as an ice cube, and Gabriel could see it on him. His eyes went soft for one long look, color creeping up his neck, and then he cleared his throat and turned back to Kim.

Kim's eyes were big, and he was grinning and fanning himself with both hands. "Is it just me, or did it suddenly get hot in here?"

"Knock it off." John looked closer. "What have you got on your face?"

One half of Kim's face was decorated with a series of stripes and jagged lines in black and white greasepaint, with one small zigzag of bright yellow cutting across the black and white. "Juan helped me do it. Isn't it hot? Do I look ferocious? Do I look like a Cheyenne Dog Soldier?"

John closed his mouth, bit down hard on his tongue. Kim's eyes were too bright, and there was a line of damp along his hairline. John thought Kim looked like he was trying too hard to cover up the marks on his face from a man's fist. He thought Kim looked like he was about to cry.

"I've decided I'm not going to be a drag queen. I can't bear the thought of this greasepaint all the time."

Gabriel handed John a cup of tea. "I think that's a good decision, Kim. Your face is plenty interesting without the paint. And you don't look like a Dog Soldier," Gabriel said. "That looks like the face paint Crazy Horse used to wear into battle. He was Oglala Sioux, not Cheyenne. I like the yellow zigzag. Like you're a lightning bolt."

"Or a lightning rod." John pulled up a chair. "How's the deposition going?"

Gabriel sighed and studied the ceiling, and Juan came over to the table to join them. "Kim, can I help make the pot stickers now?"

"Sure. Let me take you back to the kitchen. These two old ladies, they only speak Vietnamese, but just watch what they do and they'll show you. Can you cut up some green onions really small?"

"Sure! Can you stay too?"

Kim gave Gabriel a long look, trying not to grin, biting his lip. "Of course! I'm the king of pot stickers at Ho Ho's."

John drank his cup of tea, watched their retreating backs. Gabriel's eyes were travelling over his face, down his neck and across his shoulders, down to his flat belly. John had a brief image of himself crawling across the plastic tabletop, scattering noodles and chopsticks, tackling Gabriel to the sticky linoleum floor. What was it Kim had said? When you were fourteen you wanted to find a big rock and fuck it to death? When you were fifty-two, you didn't go looking for a rock.

"I could eat a steak."

John looked up, met Gabriel's eyes. The heat in his eyes seemed to scorch the air. "Yep. Me too."

The door opened, and Martha came into Ho Ho's. She looked carefully at the crying student and the sleeping homeless guy as if they were alien life forms; she studied the linoleum and the greasy handprints on the glass serving counter and the teacups on the little table.

Martha Sanchez was a proud, reserved woman. Perfect posture, her hair gathered into a shiny dark bun at the back of her neck, rosy nails perfectly manicured. She looked at Gabriel like he was somehow to blame for the seedy restaurant, maybe for the decline of the Western world, and when her eyes fell on John, they went cold. "General Mitchel." She held out her hand, and he took it. "How nice to see you." She tilted her head. "You know, Gabriel just told me recently he named our son after you. I never realized your given name was John. What was it, shared combat? Did you save his life, and I never knew? For some reason I thought it was a family name. Naturally I agreed. It's the father's prerogative to name his son, after all." She studied the surprise on his face. "You didn't know either? How interesting."

She dropped his hand and turned to Gabriel. "I've come to get Juan. Will I see you tonight?"

"Don't you always?"

"I meant for dinner." Her smile was sharp as a razor, but she kept her voice calm.

"No. I won't be home for dinner."

John cleared his throat. "Excuse me. I'll get Juan." He wasn't really sure what was going on, but Mrs. Sanchez had a couple of major thorns in her backside, and he suspected his name was on one of them. Gabriel had stayed late the last time they'd been together. Did Mrs. Sanchez wonder why they had taken so long to eat a couple of sirloins and talk about the glory days? Was that what this was about? No, couldn't be. Gabriel spent a lot of late nights working with clients or in the law library. Something else? Had Gabriel really named Juan after him? Well, Gabriel would tell him if he wanted him to know. Men had the right to some privacy. From their wives and from their lovers.

Juan looked worried when his mother pulled him out of Ho Ho's, her lips a thin line, and Kim looked worried when Gabriel carefully packed his briefcase, his face as tight as a mask. "Let's go."

John didn't ask where they were going. "You want me to drive?"

"Please." Gabriel put his seat belt on carefully.

"Let's go to my house. I've got a bottle of tequila."

"Fine," Gabriel said. "Good."

"You okay?"

He looked over then. "Not really." He hesitated. "We're having some trouble. Not your problem." He stared out the front windshield.

"You're my friend. I'm always ready to listen to a friend."

"Is that what we are? Friends? Are we more than friends?"

John didn't know what to say. Was Gabriel asking him for something, a declaration of his intentions? A declaration of his love? Had they been together too much or not enough? Kim's comments had been working their way through his mind, working their way down to his heart. *Because you've loved him for years. He's been your lover for years. It just pisses me off that you're living some kind of half-life, and dragging him into the shadows with you, just to, what, protect your reputation?* "We are friends. Friends and lovers for twenty-five years. Can you believe it's been that long?" He looked at Gabriel, reached out, and put his hand on his cheek. "You've been my only lover for all that time. The only person in the world I trust completely, besides Kim. I never wanted anyone else. Is that what you're asking me?"

Gabriel picked up his hand, pressed John's palm to his mouth. "I guess it is."

41

When they got to his house, John got the bottle of Patron Silver out of the cabinet and dug around in the fridge for something to mix with it. He found a bowl of ripe oranges on the counter and put them in the juicer with a lime. That would do. He mixed a pitcher of juice and tequila, threw in a couple of ice cubes, and brought it, and a couple of glasses, back to his bedroom. Gabriel was in the shower, his clothes neatly folded over the back of a chair. John got a coat hanger from the closet, put Gabriel's pants in the press and hung his shirt on the wooden hanger, scooted his own shirts out of the way and made a space for Gabriel's clothes in the closet. He pulled his tie off and hung it up, then poured a couple of glasses of the juice and handed one to Gabriel when he came out of the bathroom.

Water was beading across Gabriel's shoulders and chest, and his hair was wet and spiky from the towel. He had a towel tied low around his hips. He took the glass and drank half of it in one thirsty gulp. "Hey, we're teenagers again. We're gonna get shit-faced and screw till we pass out!"

"I certainly hope so." John finished his glass, then refilled both. Gabriel took a long pull, then set his glass down on the bathroom counter and gave John a little "come here" gesture with his finger. Gabriel pulled the shirt out of John's pants, pulled it down off his shoulders until it was tangled at his wrists. He gathered John's wrists in one hand, leaned over and ran his mouth down his neck until he reached the edge of his tee shirt. He took the soft cotton in his teeth, tugged it aside. Then he moved down again until he could run his tongue along John's collarbone. "We're gonna have to get this off and get down to skin."

John pulled his hands free, leaving Gabriel holding his shirt, and pulled the tee shirt over his head. Then he reached out, wrapped his hands in the top edge of the towel Gabriel was wearing. The damp hair on his chest was the same sable brown it had been twenty-five years before, still thick and lush where it trailed down his belly. John pulled the towel free, and Gabriel reached for him until they were belly to belly, mouth to mouth. It felt like it took twenty-five years for Gabriel's mouth to reach down and touch his. Then Gabriel spun him around, pressed John's back against his chest until they could see themselves in

42

the long bathroom mirror. "Look at us." He moved his hands down John's chest, slid his fingers through the hair on his chest until he could move his fingers over a bright pink nipple, then reached down and unsnapped the waistband of John's trousers. "Look at the two of us together."

His legs were long, the line of his thigh and hip strong and golden brown in the evening light. Gabriel pushed the trousers down and John stepped out of them, then stepped out of his boxers until he stood naked in front of the mirror. John leaned back against him, rested his head on Gabriel's shoulder. His skin was paler than Gabriel's, his hair lighter brown, his eyes gray and quiet as a winter sky. Just an ordinary man, nothing special to look at, until Gabriel looked at him.

Gabriel's hands moved down John's chest, down his belly, moving between his legs until he wrapped his hand around John's cock, heavy and thick in his fist. "Why shouldn't we be able to look at ourselves in the mirror every night? Every morning? John, haven't we given enough? Worked hard enough? Fuck it, what if Kim's right? Why can't we have this one small thing?"

John turned into his arms, felt the smooth skin and strong shoulders slide around him, buried his face in Gabriel's neck until he was surrounded by his smell, sweat and spice and dark wood. Gabriel smelled like something precious and rare, and he lifted John in his big arms. "Just this one thing," he said, mouth moving across John's nipple. "Is that asking too much?"

John wrapped one leg around Gabriel's hip, let their heavy cocks slide against each other. "We can have this. Take anything you want. Just don't...."

"What?"

"I can't stand to see sorrow in your eyes. It tears me up."

"I miss you, you know. Every minute when we're apart. Always have. Sometimes I think I'm going crazy with missing you."

"Yeah. Me too, Gabriel. Can you stay with me tonight? Can you tell Martha...?"

"I can stay."

CHAPTER 5

GABRIEL IN the morning was a beautiful thing, lying on his belly, long legs sprawled across the bed, face shoved down into the pillow. John slid his hand in silky dark hair. Gabriel groaned, shielded his eyes from the morning sun. And well he should, John thought, studying the level of Patron Silver left in the bottle.

Kim burst through the door, carrying a cup of coffee, and he reared back like a spooked horse at the sight of two naked men where there should only have been one. "Whoa! TMI, Uncles, TMI!"

Gabriel shoved the pillow over his head. John threw the sheet over his fine bare butt and pointed toward the door. "Out."

Kim turned to the door, eyes pinging like pinballs, biting on his lower lip to keep from grinning.

"Wait a minute. Leave the coffee. Is it hot?"

"Yeah. I made it in the Mr. Coffee. That new machine takes too long, and the French press doesn't keep it hot long enough."

"I told you that when you set it up." John took the cup, gestured toward the door with his chin. "So go get another cup!"

Kim came back with two cups, handed one to Gabriel, who had dragged himself up against the headboard. "So! Now you're both awake, can I run something by you?" He settled himself cross-legged on the end of the bed, grinning.

Gabriel turned to John. "Does he do this all the time? I mean, it's just after six, right? I never pictured him as a bright and early sort of kid."

John shook his head, never taking his eyes off Kim, who looked as delighted as a boy locked overnight in a candy store. "No, he's almost always asleep when I go for a run. Afraid I would make him join me, I always thought. I would say this is an anomaly."

Kim looked around the room, gave an exaggerated start when he spied the bottle of tequila. "Well, well, look at that! So I guess you two *are* gay, after all. I was starting to have my doubts."

John set the cup on the bedside table. "Out."

"Okay, okay, I'm sorry. I just wanted to ask you if you would come along as backup."

"Backup to what?"

Gabriel drained the coffee cup, set it down. "What do you want to do?"

"I want to go back to my favorite bar. It's not a pickup joint or anything. It's a dance bar, you know? It's where I go to see my friends. I hate not wanting to go out and be with my friends because I don't want to run into him! It's pissing me off! It makes me feel weak and stupid, and I want to stop feeling that way."

All the fun was gone from his eyes now.

"So you want us to go with? To a gay bar?"

"Uncle John, I was just going to ask you. I mean, I understand the Horse-Lord has other commitments and I don't want to get anybody in trouble. But, Uncle John, you still look like you could kick some serious ass, and I was hoping for a little…."

"For a little muscle. I get it. Sure, I'll come. Want me to wear camo? Strap on a weapon?"

Kim studied him like he wasn't sure if he was joking or not. "No, too butch. The boys would be all over you, and I don't think I could take that. A tie might be nice, you know, the professorial look. Sort of a Matrix-ninja killer in a black suit."

"Whatever that means. I'll come with you if you want, Kim."

"I'll come too." Gabriel was yawning behind his hand. "You haven't thought this out, Kim. So what if the guy's there and what if he starts hassling you? Laughing at you?" Kim's face was furious now. "You need your two big uncles to drag him into the alley and pound the shit out of him? Or we can do it in the middle of the dance floor. You want to have everybody see him with his face on the ground." The room was dead silent. "You've been thinking about it, right? How he made sure everyone looking at you pictured his mark on you. How everyone would know he did it to you. You want to do the same thing to him?"

"No, I don't! I don't want anyone to do to him what he did to me. You don't understand me at all, Horse-Lord." Kim was still furious, and John thought he heard a hint of tears in his voice.

"So explain."

"I just want to go hang out with my friends."

"With bodyguards. Okay, I'm cool with that."

"No! Not with bodyguards! I just want… I want you to help me make a quick exit if I start to lose it, okay? Don't let me embarrass myself in front of the guys."

"Then what you need is a date."

Kim covered his face with his hands and vented a tiny scream. "Please, God, give me a break from these two. You two are like so hopelessly last century."

John was grinning. "Okay, yeah, that would work. You take Gabriel out dancing, and I'll lean against the bar acting all pissed off and sullen, and whatever happens to the dickhead? Well, it's dark in gay bars, right? You bring me in, then how I deal with him is no longer your concern, Kim."

"Yes, it is my concern, and I don't want to be responsible…."

John held up a hand to stop him. "You don't have any kids, so don't tell me how I need to follow your Greenpeace PETA pacifist butt into a gay bar to *not* take care of an asshole who only understands one thing." He held up a clenched fist. "Now how about you fetch us some more of that coffee?"

Gabriel held out his empty cup without a word, and they watched Kim flounce out the door. "At least you didn't tell him he was a soft-shell crab in the middle of molting," Gabriel said. "You were kidding about the date, right?"

"Right."

"You crack me up. We're a lawyer and a professor. Our days of kicking somebody's ass in a dark bar are long over. What are we going to do, bury him in paperwork?"

"Maybe." John leaned back against the headboard and tugged on Gabriel until he rolled over, settled his head in John's lap. He reached down, brushed the silky dark hair from Gabriel's forehead. He looked happy, John thought, lighthearted and happy, like some burden he usually carried had been put down for the night. "You never spent the night with me before. You laughed in your sleep once, and it made me laugh too. I like sleeping with you."

"I did sleep with you once. Remember… where was it, Frankfurt? That was '88, I think. Or '87."

"Oh, yeah! Just outside Munich, my friend, and you tasted German sausage for the first time in a big outdoor beer garden. They kept bringing you those pints, and you were shouting, 'Another sausage! And bring one for my friend!'."

"God, those were good sausages. I don't think I've had another one since that even came close."

"I'm happy you're here. In the morning light you still look like you did when you were a baby pilot."

Gabriel reached up, traced the hair at John's temple. John knew there was a little silver visible among the brown, and he wondered if Gabriel thought he was starting to look old. "John, I've asked Martha for a divorce."

"Gabriel, I'm so sorry." He looked down into his friend's face, saw the sadness, the tiredness. "I remember how much… how much you wanted that to work. A family of your own, kids, and a real home."

"I guess I thought it was just a matter of working at it, trying hard to take care of everyone, make them all happy. It's been a hard lesson for me to swallow. That I can't succeed at the things that mean the most to me. That I can fail at something so important. But I can't change who I am, or how I feel, through force of will. And I've started to wonder… why can't I be happy too? You know, why can't I be myself? Is it really that hard? Anyway, I wanted to let you know. I'm moving out this weekend. Or sooner, if I get home and my clothes are scattered all over the street."

"Is Martha…?"

"Pissed off and feeling vindictive. Looking for someone to blame. She's gonna use the kids against me. She's already telling herself it's in their best interest."

"What did you tell her?"

"I told her I didn't love her anymore."

"Move in with me if you want. I've got plenty of room."

Gabriel shook his head. "That's not why I told you. I just wanted you to know."

"You have someone else?"

Gabriel shook his head, smiling. "No. No one else. Never anyone else."

They looked at each other then, old friends, wondering how this would change things between them. Then Gabriel smiled up at him, and John's heart turned over in his chest, and he leaned over and kissed him. *Never anyone else.* Not for either of them. He wondered if Gabriel knew how much he loved him. Maybe this wasn't the time to say it, though. His life was too complicated already.

"John, Kim might be right. I mean, his idea about how to handle this. He might be right."

"He is right. He's very perceptive, very intuitive, and he believes in redemption. I would like him to have the freedom to continue to believe in redemption for the rest of his life. I believe redemption will only occur after I crush that fucking worm under my boot heel. I don't want him to look at Kim and see weakness, not ever again. And he will, unless I bring a large deterrent to bear and shoot it up his ass."

"Agreed. So what's the current status?"

"I have a meeting with President Wainright today at eleven. I'm going to present the data I've collected and see what he plans to do. I sent him a copy a couple of days ago. The department head, the dean, and the VP have all pushed the buck upstairs. If he doesn't fire this guy immediately, I'll have to take steps."

"Would you like to have counsel present?"

"Absolutely."

GABRIEL SMILED to see his clothes hung up in John's closet, but he didn't say anything, just got dressed and went to work. He kissed John good-bye like he meant it, like he'd be thinking about that kiss all day. John was very rarely rattled by anything, but Gabriel's heat, his passion, was deeper and stronger than it had ever been, even when they'd both been very young. John felt like some volcanic rock at his center was heating up, turning hot and liquid. He turned his thoughts away from heat and flowing lava, though, and gathered up the materials he'd need for the meeting with the university president.

He'd collected statements from Kim, and from the Department Head's files on prior complaints. A report from a private investigator described four previous episodes of battery requiring medical care for three young men, none of whom decided to press changes. John had written a summary report, which included these facts, conclusions, and recommendations for action. The first of these recommendations, and the one not negotiable, was immediate dismissal from the university faculty. He had written similar reports for the Joint Chiefs of Staff, and he had no doubt Wainright would be fully cognizant of this fact, reading the current report. A copy was ready to go to the board of supervisors, which included the dickhead's father. But John would see if Wainright would act before he took that step and went over his head.

John wore a navy-blue suit made of fine Italian wool crepe that was as close to service dress blues as a suit could get and not be a uniform. His tie was red and gray stripes against a pale-gray shirt that made his eyes look like the North Atlantic in winter. People were always treated with more respect when they were dressed properly for the occasion, a lesson he had not been able to get through to Kim. Kim countered that occasions changed, but personal style was like a person's skin. John had been reminded again that Kim's soul was the color of butterflies, and he kept his tongue. The boy was still young.

Gabriel met him in the atrium of the president's office, and they walked up together. Gabriel was wearing all black, with a very white shirt and a stark, thin black tie. It made him look faintly ferocious, a predator, and John studied the shiny black shoes under the break in the cuff. "Is this what Kim was talking about? Matrix-ninja killer?"

"I think I look like one of the Men in Black." He looked at John. "Will Smith, not Tommy Lee Jones. You can be Tommy Lee Jones. You've got that stare down pat. Have had since you made Lt. Colonel. What's my role here?"

"Just back me up. Look lethal."

Gabriel nodded as the president's admin came up the hall to escort them. "Yep."

President Wainright was a big, hale, bluff sort of man who always greeted John by his military title. He'd been an amateur sailor in his youth, and was known for walking around Albuquerque wearing sailing gear. Today, though, he'd chosen to dress like a university president. "General!" He shook hands, darted an alarmed look at Gabriel, who stood silently behind John's left shoulder. "So good to see you. I don't know if I ever told you how pleased we all were when a scholar of your experience and reputation decided to join our faculty."

"Thank you, President Wainright. May I present my counsel, Gabriel Sanchez?"

"So nice to see you! You look like you might have been a military man!"

Gabriel nodded. "I'm retired from the army. I served with General Mitchel in the past."

"Really? How fascinating. You must have had a chance to travel?"

"Travel?" Gabriel was wearing his stone face, and John silently took the chair that was offered. "Lebanon, Iraq, Somalia, and Afghanistan in the ten years before law school. Some beautiful country there."

"Oh, really?" President Wainright's voice was a bit weaker. "Well, please, have a seat." He turned to John. "So, General, I understand you have a report for me to look over?"

"I sent you a copy two days ago, President Wainright, so you could have a chance to read it before the meeting today."

"Oh, yes, of course. I was able to read most of... really very concerning.... But please, call me Simon."

"Thank you. And I'm John."

Simon rubbed his hands together. "Good, fine. Now we're all comfortable, let's go through this, shall we?"

John stood up, lifted his briefcase. "Perhaps we could use the table, Simon?" He gestured to the conference table that took up the left side of the room. "There is a good bit of documentation, if you were to require it."

John laid the paperwork into four piles. "You have a faculty member who is preying on young gay men, Simon. He has a history of assault and has not been held accountable."

"John, why do you suppose, if this has been occurring, he has not been, as you say, held accountable?"

"Because the victims are young gay men, as I said. They are vulnerable in so many ways in this community, wouldn't you agree? To ask for help, or justice, may open them to greater threat. This instructor is in a position of power as a member of this faculty. His father is also in a position of power relative to this university, and this may serve to protect him."

Wainright was pale now. "Surely you are not suggesting that anyone has...?"

He stopped speaking when John lifted the first group of papers. The reports included photographs from the emergency room at University Hospital of three of the victims, and he laid these out in front of the president. "I became involved when he assaulted my nephew, Kim Baker. Kim is a graduate student at this university. I've raised him since his parents were killed in an auto accident five years ago."

"You must be very close to him. He's Korean, isn't he? Adopted from a Korean orphanage when he was a baby?"

"He's an American, Simon." John smiled, felt the other man recoil a bit. "One of your students. A student who should feel safe on this campus. A victim of a predator who has been allowed to prey on boys on your watch."

John handed over the report from the PI, then lifted the small tape recorder from his pocket and turned it on. The department head from Fine Arts spoke. "We all know what he's like, but we've never been able to make anything stick. The boys are afraid of him, and afraid to talk, you know? And he seems to be able to pick up the gentle ones, the sweet ones who won't...."

Simon frowned at the tape recorder. "Is that legal? I mean, to tape a conversation without the consent of all the parties?"

Gabriel picked up the tape recorder and played it again from the start. John's voice was clear, saying, "I'm going to record this conversation so there is no confusion later about who said...."

Simon was nodding, his hands out, patting the air. John sat silently for a moment, then handed a copy of the summary page across the table.

Simon took it. "John, what I need to explain to you is that this faculty member has, as you say, been in this situation before. Things are not quite as cut and dried as you make it seem. Now, I'm not saying any of these poor boys were complicit, but they exercised bad judgment. I know two of the boys were using drugs, and according to my professor, were equally abusive toward him. Another boy tried to steal his car, though Professor Walker never pressed charges. These incidents seem to be related to alcohol, and you know how things always seem to escalate under the influence of the grape! I'm not saying your nephew was doing anything like these other boys, but we may not have all the facts of the case. There are always two sides to these things, do you agree?"

"He is a professor at this university. He hit a student he was having an inappropriate relationship with, in the face, and he has done so before." John stood up, and Gabriel stood as well, began gathering the papers and putting them back in John's briefcase. Simon watched them with alarm. "I'm not talking to him, Simon. That will be a different conversation. I'm talking to you. I'm asking you what you will do as the leader of this community. This is not a matter two consenting adults need to work out privately."

Gabriel closed the briefcase with a sharp click and looked at John. "How long?"

John glanced at him. "Forty-eight hours?"

Gabriel nodded. "President Wainright, I will contact you then, if I may?"

CHAPTER 6

THEY WALKED across campus to John's office. John felt like he had a belly full of ice, but he also had a graduate seminar in an hour, and he was never late for his classes. Gabriel set the briefcase down next to the desk.

"What do you think?"

"He's a politician, John, not a leader. He'll try to figure out who has the most power, and who is most likely to cause him damage if he makes them an enemy. I'm not sure that's you."

"That's what I thought. Give me some options."

"Send copies of the report to all the members of the board of supervisors. Moderate chance of successful resolution. These are old boys and you're still an outsider. Powerful, with resources, but not one of them. Two, we could talk to Kim about making a police report, using the criminal justice system. Unlikely to succeed. Three, involve national authorities. The GLBT lawyers from the ACLU would climb all over this. High chance of success and Kim would have fun with all the baby lawyers. Some nice-looking boys in that group." John sighed. "Four, involve the local media. There are a couple of mad dogs who would love to sink their teeth in a nice juicy cover-up that may involve the powers that be in Santa Fe. That would end your relationship with this university fairly quickly. Five, we could...." He hesitated, and John looked up at him. "We could handle this the way we think would be most effective, and not let Kim know. Finding backup would be no problem." They exchanged a look.

"He would figure it out."

"Probably so. Six, we could let Kim figure out the way *he* wants to deal with this, and support him in his efforts."

They leaned back in their chairs and thought about the options. John shook his head. "I have always believed in trying a diplomatic solution first. But diplomatic solutions will fail when you have a failure of courage among your leadership. The follow-through is critical. A diplomatic failure will just energize this fuckhead, give him permission to do it again. That I cannot tolerate. I'll give Wainright forty-eight hours, and then we'll find another solution." He studied Gabriel. "So, how are you?"

Gabriel shrugged and smiled at him. "I'm good. Tired, probably because I was up half the night fucking my boyfriend." John stared, felt the heat start to creep up his neck, a heavy thump of lust slide down his spine. What had gotten into him? Gabriel never talked like this. "I just wanted to say that, just once. You should see your face, John. So I found a studio just a block from my office. That will be a safe and quiet place for me to ride out the storm. I have room for the kids to sleep over on a fold-down couch, but I imagine Martha is going to keep that from happening."

"How can she keep you from seeing the kids?"

Gabriel set his jaw. "She's going to say I'm homosexual, and my lifestyle isn't appropriate for them."

"How does she know that, Gabriel?"

He shook his head. "She's not a fool. I haven't been with her as much as she expected I would be, and she wants to know why. She's not like a lot of women who would blame themselves. She's blaming me, saying I kept her from having the chance to be loved by a 'real' man. That I used her to keep my military career. Maybe she's right, I don't know, John. I expect some mad-dog divorce lawyer will let me know soon enough. All I am sure about is that it's all my fault. I had, what did you call it? A failure of courage. A failure of leadership."

"You were never one of those men climbing the ladder. You didn't do it for a career. You wanted a family. Who doesn't?

Everybody wants a family, people to love, a home where you belong. Somebody waiting for you at the end of the day.

"You were doing the work the country asked you to do. It was important. And they wouldn't have let you do it if anyone had thought you were gay. Gabriel, do you remember what it was like? It's easy to forget the way it used to be, the hazing, the violence. I've not forgotten. There was work that needed to be done, and you and I were the people who needed to do it. And I would have been kicked to the curb, and so would you have been, and so would the rest of the men and women who sucked it up and kept it under cover. Lived a quiet lie, so they could serve their country. It's a new world, Gabriel, but this was never our world. It'll be better for Kim. But don't forget what it was like for us."

"You think it ever will be our world? Are we too old now to change? Let that warm sun of acceptance shine on our faces? I can't even imagine what that would be like."

John felt helpless at the longing in his friend's voice. "I don't know. Maybe the good stuff doesn't change. Maybe we could still go to Munich and eat the best sausage in the world."

That got him a smile. "I'll pencil it in. I better go. I'll call you in a couple of days, okay? When I hear back from El Presidente."

"Call me anytime. Don't forget, we're backup to a gay bar on Friday night. You don't have to come with. But it would be more fun with you there. More fun for me, I mean. But don't come if you think…."

Gabriel was biting down on his lower lip, trying not to smile. John reached out and tugged him a little closer by his black suit coat, wondering how hard it would be to change. Just a little. Enough to kiss openly, out in the world, in the sunshine. It wasn't hard at all, he discovered, and Gabriel smiled at him with tired eyes and kissed him back.

GABRIEL CALLED Friday afternoon to report that President Wainright had blown them off for the weekend. The admin, Cecilia, said he'd been "in a mood" since their visit. He also reported he was coming with them to provide Kim's backup.

Kim was excited and a little nervous, John thought, more about introducing his uncles to his favorite watering hole than anything else. Did they still call them watering holes? John wasn't sure, and he was not used to feeling so out of his element. This gay dance bar was not the Officer's Club, that much he was sure of. Kim floated into his room to check on what he was wearing. John had been instructed not to shave that morning, so he would look extra tough, but he didn't think Kim understood that whiskers coming in more gray than brown did not intimidate anyone. He'd shaved like usual.

Kim held his arms out and showed off his new tee shirt. It was black with a gold foil Buddha on the front. "It's the Compassionate Buddha," Kim explained. Then he turned around so John could read the writing on the back: *If you're new in town, follow my GREENPEACE PETA PACIFIST BUTT into this bar!*

"It was too good a line, Uncle John. I couldn't waste it."

"Out. I need to get dressed. And I need a little peace and quiet."

"So what are you wearing?"

"Out."

Kim was back in five minutes, holding a small glass of tequila through a crack in the door. John took it without a word and closed the door. It was good, he thought, taking a sip. Patron Silver, with lime juice and soda water, with a curly twist of lime peel. Kim had a knack for this.

He put on an old pair of camo pants, faded and banged up from actual use in a combat zone, black boots, and a black tee shirt. He wasn't going in looking for trouble, but he wanted trouble to take one look at him and head for the door. Gabriel knocked on his door five minutes later, holding his own glass and wearing camo pants, boots, and a dark brown tee shirt. "Hey."

John gestured with his glass. "This is good, isn't it?"

"Yeah. Not too sweet. Nice and bitter on the tongue. Kim made these?"

John nodded. "I wonder if he wants to go to cooking school."

Gabriel took a seat on the edge of the bed. "Cecilia seems to think Wainright is just trying to get an okay from somebody up the chain before he gives us any sort of reply. But I don't think she really knows what's happening. She just wanted to chat."

"You're a handsome man. I'm sure lots of ladies want a chat."

Gabriel sighed, took a sip of his drink, and John stood in front of him, pushed a knee in between his legs on the bed. "Can you come back with me tonight?"

"Sure." Gabriel looked a question at him. "If we're not in jail."

John shook his head. "It's getting pretty damn hard to sleep without you in my bed. All of a sudden, I'm staring at the ceiling in the middle of the night, wondering where you are. Wondering why I can't sleep."

"Yeah, me too. Lot of things changing, I guess."

John wondered if he was pushing too hard, or maybe not pushing hard enough? "You just tell me what you want me to do, Gabriel. What you need from me. If you need me to back off and give you some space, just tell me."

"It's not the same with you as with Martha, John. I feel like there's this lifetime of missed chances to work through. Missed opportunities. I'm not ready to peel you off with this old skin and find a new life. I liked my old life just fine." He hesitated. "Maybe I wish we could have had something more. I think back all those long years, and all I can remember is yearning and loneliness. Wondering where you were, if you were safe. When I would see you again. Waiting and waiting and waiting some more, hoping for just five minutes of your company."

John reached for his hair, slid his fingers into the silky dark. "I wonder why I've been feeling so, I don't know how to describe it, so dissatisfied. So unhappy. I mean, I'm exactly where I wanted to be. Where I planned to be. And this life feels a lot more empty than I expected it to feel. I've been thinking about you too. About all those missed chances." Gabriel looked at him, and John leaned over, tasted the cool drink on his mouth. "I know you've got a lot going on. A lot to work through. Don't let me push you into anything you're not ready for."

Gabriel tugged him back down for another kiss by a handful of his tee shirt. "I've been ready for you to push me into something for years."

Kim stuck his head in the door, gave a low wolf whistle when he saw them. "What is with you two? You're making out like teenagers every time you drink tequila."

John looked over his shoulder. "Could I suggest you not be so quick to speak when a random thought floats through your empty head?"

"Okay, fine, fine. I'm just saying. Horse-Lord, did you see my tee shirt?"

"I did. Please don't make me look at it again."

The split lip had healed, but there was still a little smudge of discoloration under his eye. John wondered if he was going to cover it up with makeup, but Kim just slid some Cherry Berry lip gloss over his mouth and stuck the tube in his pocket. "Ready, Uncles? We're going to Effex downtown. They've got a rooftop bar and a dance floor down below. You've love it."

A taxi dropped them off on Central, and Kim led the way through a group of rowdy young men and women, already partying on the street. Downtown was glitzy at night, the neon pulsing and the lights twinkling brightly, the whole scene shiny and hip. John and Gabriel walked about five steps behind Kim. He seemed to know every person on the street. He had to stop and kiss a few boys, big smacking kisses that looked like five-year-olds playing, and he let some goon in a white sleeveless tee suck on his neck while he giggled and studied the stars. He reapplied his lip gloss and pushed open the doors.

"Friend or foe?" Gabriel was studying the goon. John shrugged. They had worked out a code, a "save me code," as Kim called it. If he dropped his lip gloss onto the floor, he wanted his Uncle John. If he dropped a dollar bill to the floor, that meant he needed emergency egress. Kim had explained these signals so carefully John's heart cracked a little in his chest, remembering the baby who'd needed to be picked up and carried safely above the world.

John and Gabriel took up position next to the bar. The main floor of the club had a DJ supplying the music, and there was a second floor with a wide balcony circling the dance floor below. As far as John could see, the balcony was for strolling hand in hand, seeing and being seen. There were stairs to an outdoor rooftop bar on the third floor. Gabriel had checked it out, said it was the place for old guys like them to hang out. The music up there was straight out of 1968.

John leaned against the bar, studied the balcony, nodded at his guy watching them from above. "Everything set?" Gabriel nodded yes.

Kim floated over to them, giggling at something one of his friends was whispering in his ear. He leaned over. "I'll come tell you if I leave the dance floor, okay? Maybe later on we can go up to the rooftop? You'll like it up there. It's quieter. I know the music is kind of loud down here."

"Come get one of us before you go to the head."

Kim nodded at Gabriel, his face troubled. "That's where he did it, you know. In the men's room." His face brightened a bit. "Hey, you want to dance?"

Gabriel reared back. "God, no."

"Uncle John? How about you?"

"The bodyguards never dance."

"You can have some fun too. You don't have to watch me every minute."

"It'll be more fun watching you than anything else I could be doing tonight."

Kim gave him a look like he wasn't quite sure what John meant, then a quick hug around the waist and he plunged back onto the dance floor. Gabriel ordered them a couple of beers, and John pulled two pairs of yellow foam earplugs from his cargo pocket.

IT WAS a couple of torturous hours later when Brian Walker came onto the dance floor. John had seen pictures of him in the faculty handbook, and the PI had taken some photos as well. John touched Gabriel on the shoulder, and Gabriel moved across the floor, disappeared into the crowd on the far side of the bar. John nodded to his guys on the second floor, gave them the thumbs-up.

The man was good-looking, tall and lanky, with wavy brown hair to his shoulders. He was with a boy who looked very young, so slender he was almost frail, with wispy blond hair and a blue streak like Kim's. Kim was laughing, his arm around the shoulders of a boy with a multitude of facial piercings, Che on his tee shirt picked out in little crystals. When Kim turned around and saw Walker, he stiffened, and his hand went into his pocket, came out holding his lip gloss. He looked around for John, and his uncle gave him a little "come here" gesture with his finger. Kim hugged his friend good-bye and walked across the room. He had his lip gloss clutched in his fist so tightly that John just opened his arms, gathered him up close.

"I'm okay, Uncle John."

John looked across the room at Brian Walker, then looked over his head to the huge banner that was being unrolled from the second floor balcony. It showed a photo of Brian Walker, and Gabriel had photoshopped a black board below his head, so it looked like a mug shot. His name was picked out in bright white letters on the board, and below the image, large black letters said, "FISTS ARE NOT FOR HITTING YOUR DATES."

The dickhead looked at them, then followed John's gaze over his shoulder. He spun around, studied the image, then pointed across the room at Kim, his face livid, shading to bright red. There was a crowd of dancing kids between them, and they were stopping, looking at the banner, pointing at it and staring at Brian Walker, the sudden buzz of conversation loud in the room.

John thought they had maybe a minute, a minute thirty. Kim didn't see it, though. He had his head on John's shoulder. "I saw that Fijian boy you were dancing with earlier, Kim. Nice-looking kid. Did you tell him you'd been to Fiji?"

Kim sputtered with laughter. "Oh, God, no. Do you remember?"

"You were such a sensitive boy, such delicate sensibilities! You were reeling in the street, trying to keep from retching, a handkerchief over your nose, and you kept saying, 'My God! Sewers *and* dumpsters *and* the fish market!'."

"I can still smell it. I thought, if I lost you and got stuck on that street, I would just die. If you disappeared, and I was alone there...."

"You won't lose me."

"That was just after Mom and Dad died. I guess I was thinking about what life would be like, to be a street kid in the third world. That might have been my life, if Mom hadn't brought me home from Seoul."

John didn't know what to say. He'd had no idea Kim still thought about the past like that, still had fears he could be thrown back like a fish that was too small for market. "You about ready to go?" He stroked Kim's back, kept his head down.

"Where's the Horse-Lord?"

"I think he went to the head."

Kim straightened, looking across the crowded dance floor. He saw the banner and stiffened. He was trying not to make eye contact with the dickhead, and he still had his lip gloss in his hand. "Oh, my God! What is that?"

Brian Walker was struggling through the crowd, making for them. John reached out, tugged him back into his arms, wrapped him up tight. "I love you, kiddo. Have I told you lately?"

Kim turned around and looked at him in surprise. "I love you too, Uncle John. Do you know anything about that banner? You didn't do that, did you?" He was looking at his uncle, a question on his face, and he missed the crack of a boot on the side of a knee. Brian Walker screamed, took a header, and slid across the dance floor, plowing into startled boys and girls until he ended at the bottom of a pile of shrieking arms and legs. He screamed, clutched his knee, then his contorted face turned to John. John slung his arm across Kim's shoulder, kept him from rushing out to the dance floor. "They don't need your help, son."

He had Kim by the sleeve, pulled him gently through the crowd until they were outside. Gabriel was waiting for them on the sidewalk.

He turned, handed John his pair of yellow foam earplugs. "Those things really work. I could use a pair of those in court."

Kim studied them both. "What just happened in there? Did you do that? I didn't see what happened. Uncle John, I told you I didn't want you to do anything."

"The only reason I didn't do serious damage to that dickhead was to spare your sensitive feelings. And I reserve the right to change my mind about that." John reached out, pulled the little tube of lip gloss from his hand. He pulled the lid off, took a sniff. "This cherry isn't as bad as that one you used to wear. What was it? Watermelon? The smell drove me crazy."

Kim took it back, stuffed it into his pocket. He was moving between outrage and laughter. "Watermelon and green apple. I have every intention of buying a new tube tomorrow."

CHAPTER 7

KIM STAYED at home most of the weekend, but avoided him, and Gabriel spent Saturday moving out of his house. They had both agreed without speaking that it was probably better if John and Kim didn't help him move boxes of his clothes to his pickup truck. He came back to John's to sleep Saturday night, and was so miserable and restless in bed John finally pulled him outside to help him with the hot tub. John had a high fence around the back yard, and they worked together without speaking to fill the tub in the middle of the night. They turned on the heater and drank tequila until the water was warm. They climbed into the tub about four in the morning. Gabriel finally laid back, his head on an orange life vest, and floated in the warm water. John watched over him, watched the tears that slid down his face while he slept.

Sunday morning Gabriel drove off to his new studio apartment. The place looked to John like a seedy extended-stay hotel, and he wondered if Gabriel was making himself miserable as some kind of penance.

He was ready to go back to work Monday just to escape the gloomy house. Still no word from the president about what he intended to do, and John had decided to give him until the end of business Monday. Monday afternoon, just after lunch, he looked up to see Brian Walker balancing on crutches in his office doorway. He had an enormous padded splint on his left leg, looked like he couldn't bend the knee. John studied him without speaking.

"Just so you know, I haven't said anything about this. I know you did it. I wanted to be clear with you that this makes us even. I didn't realize Kim had such an overly protective Uncle John! General John Mitchel, to some people. Who knew?"

"I might suggest you start packing," John said. He sat behind his desk and folded his hands. The other man remained standing. "When you are out of this university and out of this town, we can discuss equity again."

Brian Walker's face was shading dark red, and he snarled, showing his teeth. John suspected this was the face Kim had seen, the other boys too, right before he'd raised his fist and punched them in the face. "You don't know who you're fucking with, *General*. You think you're so important and powerful?"

John stood up, walked around the desk. "You can leave this university now before things get ugly. This is your last friendly warning." Brian looked confused for a moment. John shook his head. "This was nothing, just a little love tap. You pick up your boys there? Or in your classes, professor? Somehow I doubt that boy you were with is old enough to drink. Is he even legal?"

"I don't have to pick them up in class. They come to me. Kim was practically humping my leg, he was so ready to fuck, bending over for it like a little Korean dog."

John could feel the corruption coming off the man, like the faintest odor of something rotten under the sweet-heavy aftershave. He remembered for one clear moment Kim's face when he was a year old, spotting him across the orphanage floor, two front teeth, drool on his chin, and crawling across the room as fast as his skinny arms and legs could carry him. The clean, bright, delightful smell of his baby filled his memory, and he'd pounded Brain Walker in the mouth twice, had him down on the floor with blood smearing his chin, before he could draw a breath.

Cynthia came in the door, her hand pressed tightly over her mouth, but John waved her away. "This doesn't make us even. I could spend the rest of my life kicking your corrupt ass and it wouldn't begin to make us even. Now get the fuck out of my office."

Brian struggled to his feet, his hands so tight on the crutches his knuckles were white. Blood was smeared across his face and down his shirt, and his mouth was torn. He stopped at the door like he might want to say something in parting, but John was back behind his desk, working.

He got a call from Gabriel just after the dickhead left. "El Presidente wants to see us, and so does Kim. He asked if I could fetch you and meet at Ho Ho's for dinner."

"Oh, God. I can't imagine that place at dinnertime. Listen, can I give you some money to put aside in case we need bail? I don't want to call Kim if I get arrested."

"Did you assault someone?"

"Yeah. And there was a witness."

"That's too bad," Gabriel said. "But unlikely to come to anything. He's a coward. He does his dirty work in the dark. He wouldn't run the risk of getting the police looking into his business."

"I agree. But I'll give you some emergency egress funding just in case."

"I told Kim we'd be there at four for soup. I'm on my way to your office now to pick you up."

"I'll meet you outside."

They walked to the president's office and said hello to Cecilia, who greeted them with some reserve on her face. John took this as a sign, and this was confirmed when Simon didn't stand up to greet them when they walked in. "Gentlemen! Thank you for coming at such short notice. Have you met Gregor Korbel? He's counsel for the university."

Gregor was a mild-looking man, and Gabriel greeted him like an old acquaintance, asked after his wife.

"Good, good. I'll have her call Martha, we'll get together for dinner."

"Sounds great." Gabriel smiled, then took John's briefcase and sat at the conference table. He pulled out a file folder that contained one page. John stood behind a chair, waiting for Simon to get down to it.

"General, please have a seat. I've showed your report and evidence to counsel, as well as to a couple of select members of the board of supervisors to get their opinions. It seems as if this issue is not as cut and dried to other people as it is for you. One solution that was offered by Board members would be that we could offer alcohol education and treatment to the boys involved, in the hopes they would not keep getting into these uncomfortable situations. Also, it appears these incidents all occurred off campus, which significantly...."

John turned to Gabriel, and Gabriel took the paper out of the folder and passed it across to the president. John stood up. "President Wainright, I appreciate you hearing my concerns about this matter. My resignation is effective immediately. The department head will find all notes relevant to my classes on my desk. The students have assignments through next week they can complete independently, so you will have time to find a replacement."

"General Mitchel! Surely this isn't necessary! I understand you're taking a stand on this matter to support your adopted nephew, but to resign over this...."

Gabriel stood, and when John nodded, he opened the office door. "Gregor, good to see you. President Wainright, thank you for seeing us."

They walked across campus to John's office, where Gabriel had left his truck. Gabriel put John's briefcase behind the seat. "About what we expected. First salvo across the bow."

John flexed his hand. "I'm getting too old to punch people in the mouth. My hand hurts like a bitch. So what's happening at Ho Ho's?"

"I'm not sure. How was Kim this weekend?"

"Still in a snit."

"He said Juan was coming to help with the pot stickers after class, so that will make two of them in snits. I can't wait."

"Should be fun."

Kim and Juan were at the prep table behind the smudged glass serving counter, dealing with a mountain of celery and green onions. Gabriel and John leaned over the counter to get a look at Juan's new haircut, a very sharp, very short high and tight, with the front left long enough for a wavy blond streak. He pretended not to see them for a few moments, the color creeping up the back of his neck, but Kim was incapable of not showing off. "Oh, my God! Horse-Lord, he's so handsome! He's going to be a model. He's going to be in a band. He'll be so famous he won't even know us. He'll be on a yacht in the Mediterranean with Madonna and Donatella Versace and all we'll be able to do is wave good-bye from the shore when he sails off to fame and fortune."

John wasn't sure what all that nonsense meant, but he was happy it got them through a few awkward moments.

"You two, go sit at the table. We've made your soup and tea." He leaned over, whispered something to Juan, and the boy burst out laughing. His neck was bright red now.

Gabriel took John's arm and they went to a clean table. "Whatever he just said, I have a feeling it was about us! Always happy to bring a little comic relief, if I can't do anything else. Think he'll be bringing us soup at Ho Ho's when we're eighty-five and can't remember our way home?"

"Count on it, my friend."

Their tea was brought by one of the old women from the pot-sticker fight. She seemed gentle today, gentle and sad. "Thank you for letting Kim do his art project in the restaurant," John said. "He's very excited."

"It will be very good, very good," she said, adjusting the fold of a tiny napkin. John could see her arms were riddled with old scars, burn scars, like most cooks had, and some ancient linear scars on the underside of her forearms, old defense wounds. The injuries a person got when they raised their arms to cover their face when someone was hitting them. She patted him on the shoulder with a tiny hand, and Juan carried two soup bowls to the table and put them down. He avoided looking at either of them, and Kim was next with a covered tureen.

John looked at him when he put the bowl down. "So are we going to hear the details about this art project?"

Kim waved his hands around like he was fanning the flames. "Don't worry about that now! Just have your soup and tea. And then we'll talk." Of course he couldn't stop himself. "You're going to love this, I swear! My best idea all year."

The soup was excellent again, a smoky cream of mushroom, and the boys waited behind the counter, working on the evening prep, while they ate. When John pushed his empty bowl away, accepted the cup of tea Gabriel poured, he looked at their backs, wondered what they were up to. Juan came to clear the table and brought them two fortune cookies. "Dad, Mom said to call her when you were done eating."

John opened his cookie, read the fortune out loud. "'And where the offence is, let the great axe fall.' Hamlet." He frowned at the slip of paper. Hamlet? He looked at Gabriel "What does yours say?"

Gabriel broke open the cookie, read the paper out loud. "'Life being what it is, one dreams of revenge.' Paul Gauguin. Huh. Weird. Are these literary quotes fortune cookies?"

"You don't think Kim…?" He looked behind him at the kitchen. "No. No way."

Gabriel stood, took the phone out of his pocket, and waved Juan over to the table. "Is everything okay at home? Your sister?"

Juan stood like a baby tree, sighed, and stared down at the floor. "I don't know, Dad. Everybody's mad all the time. Martie's acting like a baby. We don't like that you're gone."

"I miss you guys a lot."

Juan studied his face for a moment, and when he'd stepped outside to call Martha, Juan sat down in his seat. He looked across the table at John. "Mom said you knew my dad even before she did."

"I met your dad in 1983. We were in Beirut, just after the bombing of the Marine Corps barracks. Then in 1986 we met again. We were on our way to Africa. There was a war on back then."

Juan was nodding. "I saw that movie, *Black Hawk Down*."

"What did you think about it?"

"It was kind of scary, since my dad used to fly helicopters. I kept thinking about if that had been him."

"He's never been shot down. He saved my life more than once in a helicopter, though. I think anyone but him at the controls, and we both would have…. Anyway, did he ever tell you about the time the missile nearly hit us?"

Juan shook his head.

"We were in Africa again. Not Somalia, but close, and I had a meeting with a tribal leader who was thinking about letting us build a dam on a little river across his land. Your dad took us into the mountains, stood by for security, and took us back after the meeting. This was just after you were born, because he had a little picture of you on the instrument panel, you and your mom. The first SAM nearly hit us. You know what a SAM is?"

"Surface-to-air missile?"

"That's right. Those are not very accurate when fired from somebody's shoulder, from a jury-rigged handheld launcher, and they leave a big smoke signature. So we could see where he was, and where he was firing from. Your dad, he flew that chopper like it was smoke, a widening spiral up in the air," John used his finger to show Juan the pattern, like a little funnel cloud. "His squadron called themselves the Horse-Lords of Rohan, after the great horse tribes of Middle Earth. *The Lord of the Rings*," he explained to Juan's blank face. "His chopper was painted like a great silver-white warhorse with a long, black mane. He was so mad somebody tried to shoot him down. His teeth were clenched shut. Then he was yelling from the cockpit, 'Are you kidding me? I've got a new baby boy at home I've never even seen. No way are you shooting me down before I get to hold my son!' I knew right then nothing was as important to him as you."

"Is that really true?"

"Ask him. Whenever I had to go into hostile territory, to try and work deals for new roads or new bridges with the tribes that owned the land, I always wanted your dad to be my pilot. I knew he would get us home safely."

"That's what you did? You built roads and bridges?"

71

"Mostly. Later on my job was tactics and strategy. And leadership. Sometimes the very best strategy is to make friends of your enemies. That doesn't always work, though." He thought briefly about Brian Walker, bleeding on his office floor, standing over him with a clenched fist. He flexed his fingers under the table. "Are you thinking about the army?"

"Not really. The Marines seem pretty cool."

John closed his eyes briefly, tried not to picture Gabriel's face if he heard this.

"Have you killed a lot of people?" Juan asked.

"How many is a lot?"

Juan shrugged. "More than twenty? Kim's thinking about becoming a Buddhist, though, so he says even killing an ant would do harm that shakes the universe down to its soul."

"Really. What do you think about becoming a Buddhist?"

"That would mean, like, giving up chicken tenders. Forever. That's burgers and pepperoni and sausage on pizza. I don't know if cheese would count. I mean, cows aren't harmed when they make cheese, right?"

"Not that I know of, but there may be a unique Buddhist perspective on cheese. We'll check with Kim."

Gabriel came back in, joined them, and put his hand on Juan's shoulder. "I need to take you home, buddy. Mom says we have a parent-teacher conference tonight. A special parent-teacher conference with the math teacher."

Juan winced and scooted back his chair, pulling the apron over his head "Okay, Dad."

"Anything you need to tell me before I go in? Always helps to have full disclosure before the teacher gets her say."

"Um...."

John stood up. "Gabriel, I'll get a ride home with Kim. I'll talk to you later, okay?"

"I'll see if I can come up with some options for the next step. And we need to talk to Kim, see what he thinks. I think we need to hear how he would proceed with this before we do anything else."

"Yeah, okay. I'll see what he has to say. Juan, I'll see you next time. I like your haircut. Very USMC."

"Bye, General Mitchel."

Gabriel looked up, then shook his head like his hearing was going bad. "USMC?"

GABRIEL SLEPT somewhere else. John stared up at the ceiling, noticed the cobwebs in the corner of the bedroom about 0200, and got the broom out of the pantry to deal with them. While he was up there, he ran a damp paper towel over the upper edge of the window frames and the doors. Maybe Martha had asked him to reconsider, to spend the night and try to make things work. Gabriel was emotionally fragile right now. He could be manipulated into almost anything by thinking the kids needed him at home. And of course he still cared for Martha. She was a fine person, strong and resolute in a way that had always appealed to Gabriel.

Twenty-five years, and John had never before had any expectations. He'd never waited for someone who wasn't coming. He put the work first, had always assumed he would be alone, and so he was never disappointed. When Gabriel had been able to join him for dinner, share a steak and a couple of hours of his company, it was like an especially beautiful sky on a sunny day. Now the possibility existed for something more. Gabriel had started whispers of longing deep in his chest—*why can't we have this*—while he was running his strong hands over John's skin. John had started wanting something he'd never allowed himself to want before, and here he was lying in bed, staring at the ceiling, wondering where Gabriel was spending the night.

Kim knocked on his closed bedroom door, then stuck his head inside. "I didn't see the Horse-Lord's truck outside. You okay?"

"Of course I'm okay. It's not like I haven't been sleeping alone every night for my entire adulthood." He sounded cranky and tired as a toddler.

Kim crawled into bed, pushed the pillow under his head. "So you really miss him, huh? Seems like things are changing between you two."

"I don't know. Neither one of us really knows...." John sighed, put his arms behind his head. "It doesn't seem to me that human relationships ever get easier, no matter your age and experience. So don't count on that, okay?"

"Okay." Kim curled up, stared at the side of John's head until he rolled over and looked at him.

"Yes?"

"I want to talk about what happened at Effex."

"Okay. So talk."

"It appears, though I find it hard to believe, that you made a sign with an obscene gay joke. And Brian was hurt. He's walking around on crutches, giving everyone, especially me, dirty looks."

"Why are you still in his class? I can't believe you don't have another option."

"Uncle John, he was hurt."

"So what? So were you. And I suspect your hurts are going to run deeper than his. Kim, he doesn't understand anything except power. You do get that about him, right?"

Kim nodded. "But why does that have to be our response? Doesn't that just put us on his level?"

John shook his head. "The warrior-philosopher brings a number of weapons to the negotiation. We're still negotiating. And Gabriel made the sign. I'm sure any joke was unintentional."

Kim rolled his eyes. "Why exactly are you doing this negotiating for me like I'm still a kid? Why can't I handle this?"

"I am the king. You're the knight sitting at my round table. That's the nature of our relationship when it comes to war or other conflict resolution in this family."

"If you'd said I was the samurai, and you were the shogun, I was going to get up and leave this bed."

"If you have classes tomorrow, maybe you better get to sleep. You smell like beer and cigarette smoke and cherry lip gloss."

"I went out with my friends after work. Everybody knows what's going on now, thanks to your Photoshop work, so the guys say they'll look out for me. You have morning classes, don't you? I don't have to get up until eleven."

"I have the day off." John could have bit his tongue when he realized what he'd said.

Kim was all over it. "A day off? No way. How come?" John didn't say anything, his tired brain scrambling for a reason that was not exactly a lie. "Uncle John, what did you do?"

"I gave the president my letter of resignation." Lying was a weak strategy that always backfired.

"You're not happy teaching your classes? But you would never just walk away in the middle of the semester. Does this have something to do with what happened to me?" Kim was keeping his voice very calm, but his fists were clenched on the bedspread.

"Only in a very tangential sense."

"Really."

"Kim, do you think I would ever be associated with a university faculty that knowingly harbored a pedophile, shielded him from justice and left kids at risk? Or a murderer?"

"No, of course not."

"But it would be okay to be associated with a faculty that looked the other way for other types of violence? Are we going to say this violence is understandable, a minor sort of violence, not that big a deal, the boys were drinking, they were probably asking for it, they aren't going to make a fuss. They're just gay boys, after all, and he's a professor. He's a powerful man's son. He has importance that those boys don't have. Are we under the impression I would look the other way if I knew about this happening to someone else's son? That's what I mean about the tangential association."

"Hmmm." Kim sighed. "Actually, I think you would fight for any victim who needed protecting, but you'll fight extra hard for the victims you happen to love."

"Okay, agreed."

"The thing is, I don't want to be a victim. 'Victim' is not an idea I'm going to let take root in my head."

"So don't be a victim. Figure out what you need to do. I'm trying to make sure this university does the right thing, which is my responsibility as a member of the faculty. And if they won't, I will not remain a faculty member. That's fairly simple. Your part in this is different. Tell me what I can do to help and I'll help. But you've always been a self-sustaining kid. You'll figure out how to keep your colors bright."

"I do have a few ideas," Kim admitted. "What are you going to do with this day off tomorrow?"

"I have an article I need to finish for *Foreign Affairs*, but I've been thinking about building a cold frame in the back yard," John said. "Growing some spinach and lettuce."

"Really."

"Maybe some basil. You've been experimenting with food and drink a lot lately. Are you thinking about moving on from photography? You want to go to cooking school?"

Kim shook his head. "No, I don't think so. I'm just playing around. Though if you want to start growing veggies in the backyard, maybe you can put in some dinosaur kale. I saw a great recipe for bean soup, white beans and dino kale."

"Does dinosaur kale need an extra-large cold frame? We better find out before I buy the wood."

"Want me to tell you a bedtime story?"

John rolled over again, looked at him. "What kind of bedtime story?"

"It's a romance. I call it 'The General and the Horse-Lord'. It has a happy ending, of course. All the great love stories have happy endings."

John rolled to his back, stared at the ceiling some more, wondered where Gabriel was sleeping.

"Don't you want to hear it, Uncle John?"

"I'm spending more time thinking about the past than I am the future," he admitted. "I'm not sure if our love story is so tangled up in the past that it can't grow into the light. Maybe Gabriel is going to have to chop down everything, dig out the roots, and start his life new. That's what most men do, seems to me. When they get divorced and start on the rest of their lives."

"He's never been like most men. I think he's going to make his own rules. And your job is to stay calm. Stay the course. Keep the fires burning. Be a place he can come to see himself. He needs to see himself in the reflection in your eyes. He wants to be the man you see when you look at him." Kim gave a theatrical shudder. "It's so smoking hot, when the two of you look at each other."

"Love stories usually start with a meeting, not a divorce. I don't know if I believe in love stories or happy endings, Kim, not in this world. Not in the world where I live. What I do believe is we all do the best we can do. We have to adjust our expectations to the reality of the situation."

"Uncle John, that's not good enough, not when you're talking about love. You've spent too many years adjusting your expectations down, down, down. You have to have faith in what's between you. You have to be able to risk your heart."

"You're just a baby. You're repeating this nonsense you've heard, and you see the real world through the silly gossamer fabric of your desire for happy endings. Would you ask him to choose between the good of his children and the desire in his heart? The desire for peace and companionship, the desire to sleep with someone he loves? How does that compare with the needs of his children, with his wife, a woman who has always been strong and faithful and stood beside him? He's never been a man to walk the easy path, or put his own needs above the needs of others. Neither have I."

"Juan knows perfectly well what's going on."

"You haven't said anything to him, have you, Kim? You need to stay out of their business."

"He's a nice kid and he needs to talk. He told me they've been fighting for a year, and she's always mad and he's always finding excuses to leave the house. The Horse-Lord goes out running and he runs for an hour and then he sits on the front porch, exhausted and sweaty, like he doesn't want to come inside. Juan also said she accused him of having an affair. With you. It took him awhile to figure out what she was talking about."

John sighed. "Martha isn't stupid. And the army is a small community. We've been friends for so long. He was my favorite pilot for years. Everybody knew that, but I never heard any talk that went beyond the line. But who knows? Maybe I would have been the last person to hear gossip. He had his own career. He made CW-5 before he retired, but he never wanted to lose his horse and take a desk job." John pushed the pillows flat, closed his eyes. He was getting weary.

"What if the university won't cave in and take you back?"

John winced. "It's not caving in. It's understanding that men of integrity care enough to do the right thing. If they won't *cave*, as you say, I won't even consider going back. And frankly, it hasn't been what I had hoped for. There is not a community of scholars here, not in my field. I guess that's what I was planning for when I retired. Hoping for."

"You going to write? All those articles and book chapters people keep asking you to write? Why don't you write some textbooks on leadership? Or go with one of those think tanks up in DC that wanted you?"

"Maybe I will. But you'll have to come. I can't have you racing around Albuquerque with a yellow zigzag painted on your face, and me not here to supervise your every move."

"And now Gabriel will have to come too."

John closed his eyes. He would never ask Gabriel to leave his family. And it wasn't up to him, in any case. Maybe he was not even a variable in Gabriel's equation. And where was he sleeping tonight?

"So the Horse-Lord moved to Albuquerque because Mrs. Horse-Lord wanted to come, and you moved here because he was here, and I came because of you. Now we're going to have to go in reverse. I think that means I get to pick the next place. Then you follow me, and he follows you..." Kim sighed. "Man, it is complicated, loving people. Especially when you keep pretending to be old army buds, nothing else. No bedtime story for you. Not until you admit you believe in the power of love."

"In that case I'll just go to sleep. And you need to wash the cigarette smoke out of your hair before you go to bed. Otherwise you'll have to wash your pillowcases tomorrow. All this secondhand smoke can't be good for you."

"I love you, Uncle John."

"Me too, kiddo." It wasn't until Kim was back in his little apartment in the garage that John thought about what the woman at Ho Ho's had said, something about Kim's art project. Kim still hadn't told him what was going on.

CHAPTER 8

IT WAS after one before Gabriel called and saved him from his cold frame project. "Hey, John, can I bring my tools over and store them in your tool shed? I have more than I thought I did. They fill up most of the floor space in my new studio apartment."

"I really wish you would. And you can help me finish this cold frame."

"You're building a cold frame? How come?"

"Lettuce," he said, his voice clipped. "And to be accurate, I am *failing* to build a cold frame. I am *giving up* on building a cold frame."

"You need a level and a good T square," Gabriel said. "Both of which I have. I'll come after work, okay? Do you have any sawhorses? I have two, currently sitting next to my bed. I have a toolbox where your pillow should be."

He sounded good, John thought. The parent-teacher conference must not have been too bad. "Okay. We'll definitely need the sawhorses. And I'll take a nap like an old man with nothing to do until you get here."

"Retirement becomes you, General. Want me to bring some steaks?"

"Yes, I do."

"Okay, then."

GABRIEL'S TOOLS filled most of the back of his pickup. He'd stopped and changed before coming over, was wearing jeans and a tee shirt that said *Life is Good.* John opened the door to the shed and they unloaded the tools.

"This is the neatest shed I've ever seen." Gabriel put aside what they needed for the cold frame, studied the cut pieces of plywood on the workbench. "You're doing pretty good. It's just hard to put together a project that has right angles with only one person. You need one to hold and one to put the screws in."

"Is this everything?" There was plenty of room. Gabriel's tools only took up half the shed.

"I've got a bag of charcoal and my ditty bag in the front seat."

John reached in the front seat of the truck, felt a little tenderness when he picked up the battered leather bag. Military men always carried ditty bags with their toothbrushes, their razors and personal gear. He'd seen Gabriel's so many times, sitting next to his own on a bathroom shelf. He carried it into the bathroom off his bedroom, moved his shaving gear over so Gabriel could have his own space on the bathroom counter. He stared down at it, wondered if he would be so lucky to see it in the morning. Maybe even every morning. Wouldn't that be something. "God's in his heaven, and all's right with the world."

Gabriel had brought a suit bag too, and John hung his work clothes up in the closet, then went into the kitchen and started pulling the salad ingredients out of the fridge. Gabriel had turned on the little CD player out on the back porch, was listening to Bruce Springsteen sing "Devils & Dust." John could hear the sound of a hand drill and the music, and Gabriel singing along. Kim was off to work, and he'd taken his cameras with him for a little night photography at Effex. John thought he'd try to make blue cheese dressing for their salad.

Gabriel came into the kitchen an hour later. "Done."

"What, the whole thing is done?"

"Yep. We just need potting soil and a place with morning sun. It doesn't need a bottom. We put a little gravel down and the pots on top."

"How did your parent-teacher conference go last night? Juan okay?"

Gabriel washed his hands in the kitchen sink. "Yeah, he's okay. The teacher said it wasn't anything like a character issue. He's trying, and he's not acting up in class. She recommended a tutor. Martha was thinking about one of those places like Sylvan Learning Center. But Juan says his teacher moonlights at Sylvan. I don't know. That has the appearance of a conflict of interest to me."

"It might be nice for him to have some one-on-one time with the teacher. Shame you have to pay for that."

"What do you think about finding some hungry grad student?" Gabriel pulled out a kitchen chair and watched John at the cutting board.

"Well, you've really got the luck of the draw. They all know their algebra, but do they know how to teach it?" John thought a moment, picked up the chopped tomatoes, and put them in the salad bowl. "Gabriel, you remember I have a degree in engineering? That was like a hundred years ago."

"Yeah, I remember." He was grinning. "Sometimes, when we were deployed, you would get in a particularly *thoughtful* mood. You probably don't know this, but your eyes can get really silver-looking when you're pissed. Most of the time they just look calm, you know? Zen calm. But when there was a major fuckup, they'd go really silver. And the guys, they'd say, uh-oh, General Mitchel, he must be doing some math in his head. Or, the general must be getting ready to do some calculations."

John looked at him in surprise. "Huh. Who knew?"

"The guys thought it was kind of cool you were an egghead, but still really kick-ass."

John suspected when Gabriel was talking about the guys, he really meant himself. But that was pretty cool too.

"If you want, I can do some tutoring with Juan. It might not be a bad idea for him to have some one-on-one time with the teacher, but she's already not been successful teaching him, you know? Maybe another way of presenting the same material will be more successful that just one person going over the same thing again. But I don't know if it would make Martha feel uncomfortable."

"She was better last night. Didn't seem to hate me quite so much."

"That's good."

Gabriel stood up and slung an arm around John's shoulder. "It's good to be with you. I like your company. Have I told you that?"

"Yes. I like your company too. I like having your tools in my shed." John reached down, tugged Gabriel closer with his fingers tucked inside the waistband of his jeans. "I most definitely like having you in my bed at night."

"I couldn't sleep with my arm around a metal toolbox last night. The pillow smelled like grease and rust. Not like you." He nuzzled a little under John's ear. "Let me talk to Martha. I feel like I'm willing to do whatever she wants, just to keep any small peace, but I'll tell her you offered. Juan thinks you're cool."

"Juan likes me to tell him stories about his father."

WHEN THE steaks and salad had been eaten, and John was clearing the table, Gabriel got his briefcase and opened it. "We need to consider some options," he said, and his grin looked particularly wolfish. "I wonder what the endgame is. Do you want to take these pricks to their knees, or would you like to get the job done quietly? And where do you see yourself at the end?"

"And I wonder if you are going to start charging me for your legal services?"

Gabriel nodded yes. "From the first trip into the president's office. Before that I was just being Kim's Uncle Horse-Lord. I can give you the family rate."

"That sounds good." John studied the smooth surface of the table. "Actually, I think I want to meet the dickhead's father. If he's manipulating the functioning of the university for personal reasons, up to and including protecting an abusive son, then he needs to be off the board of supervisors. I still don't know what Kim's planning."

"So we have two issues of concern. The first is an abusive professor on the university faculty. The other is the apparent unwillingness of leadership at the university to address this behavior appropriately. A corollary to the second is the possibility that this inappropriate protection goes up to the board of supervisors."

"Do we know who Wainright gave a copy of the report to on the board of sups?"

Gabriel shook his head. "Not for sure, but I would assume Brian Walker's father. Plus Cecilia mentioned 'she' had received a copy of the report, and there are only two women on the board. But it doesn't matter. You don't go to the board. You go over their head. Dr. Charles Lathrop recruited you into academia when you retired?"

"He did." John studied Gabriel's handsome face. "And now he's Governor Martinez's cabinet minister for education."

"If I was the head of education in New Mexico, I would rather not hear about this from the newspaper."

"He's a political appointee, though. The board has the power, control of the money. He does have a role in hiring and firing the senior executives if he wants to use that power, but it's rarely done." John sighed. "I don't know, Gabriel. I don't really have much interest in going back into the classroom. I'm not accomplishing anything there. Maybe I need to take my resignation off the table and let's just get this job done, get Brian Walker out of the university."

"You don't want to go back? What do you want to do?"

John looked up. "I don't know. I've been used to doing work that mattered. Now I'm just...."

"You're feeling like Ulysses. 'It little profits that an idle king, By this still hearth, among these barren crags, Matched with an agèd wife, I mete and dole Unequal laws unto a savage race, That hoard, and sleep, and feed, and know not me.' If you want to go up to Santa Fe and see Lathrop, I can take you in my chopper."

"Like old times." John smiled to see the eagerness in Gabriel's face. "What's this one called?"

"Torii Motoada. He died a beautiful death in service to his shogun. It's my last warhorse."

"Why's it the last?"

"I'm going to have to sell it, John. Too expensive to keep up with the maintenance and insurance. I need to make sure the family has everything they need. They'll keep the house. I'm thinking about giving Martha my retirement."

"The whole thing? Seems like a lot, your equity in the house and your entire military pension."

"It won't be enough, not with the kids. I don't want them to have to change anything else. I mean, that way should be easiest on them, right? Life goes on, and they just see me a bit less often, like I was deployed."

"I'm sorry, Gabriel."

He shook his head. "It's going to be worth it in the end. But come out with me one more time before I have to sell the pony, okay?"

"I'll always ride with you."

JOHN WAS already in bed when Gabriel found the book and brought it in. "I knew you'd have Tennyson on your shelf. I've been thinking about Ulysses. I always thought it was about a warrior after the war, but it's more than that. It's about what it feels like to get old. I think that's how you're feeling, stuck doing work you don't believe in. Listen to this: 'How dull it is to pause, to make an end, to rust unburnished, not to shine in use!'"

"Yep. That about covers it."

"This is the line I love: 'Yet all experience is an arch wherethrough gleams that untraveled world, whose margins fade for ever and for ever when I move.' I've always loved the moving. I could see it just ahead, the next place, mountains with new crags, little hidden lakes blue as mirrors, and the stars, new stars scattered across the sky, different stars from the ones at home. The new things I could see in my warhorse, when we took to the sky. I feel like a poet." Gabriel moved his hand up to his throat. "I don't have the words of the poets, but I have the feelings. Maybe everyone does."

"I loved the moving too. But for me it was the challenge of the work. Learning how to get things done. The new cultures, the new religions, the new languages. Like learning the steps of a beautiful and complicated dance."

Gabriel put the book next to the bed and climbed in between the sheets. He reached out, touched John's face, moved his fingers down across his forehead, traced the line of his nose. "You don't even realize it, do you, how good-looking you are? You have one of those faces that keeps getting better looking with age."

"I have a boring, ordinary face. Nothing you say can change that. It's been helpful, actually, in my work. I'm frequently overlooked by men who are taller and more physically powerful."

"That's a mistake."

"Yes, it is. You're the handsome one in this bed. Tall, dark, and dangerous." Gabriel grinned at him. "I know, I'm not a poet either. But I have the feelings of a poet. Half the squadron used to watch you walking into the hanger, looking at your bird, rolling on your feet like your balls were titanium steel. I've seen men drool when you bent over to look in the cockpit."

"If I was walking around with titanium balls, then I'd just had a briefing and been told I was going to take General Mitchel into a war zone, and don't fuck it up and get him killed, please."

"You happy with the law? Do you like what you're doing?"

"Fair. I thought I would hate the paperwork, but I'm slowing down. I don't mind so much the time at a desk. I really like the strategy. It's a war game. Not like the real thing, but close enough for my retirement years. I'm shooting money instead of real weapons. That's okay, I guess, for an arthritic old pilot."

"Are you getting arthritis?"

"My left knee hurts like a bitch when I run," Gabriel said. "I've been walking on the treadmill, if you can believe that shit."

"Maybe we can go hiking in the foothills." Gabriel was grinning at the ceiling again. "What?"

"This. You and me, talking things over before we go to sleep."

"You're probably used to having somebody to talk to before you fall asleep," John said.

"Lately, there's been this wide, deep space between us, and neither one of us wanted to bring up anything to start a fight. So we'd just lay in the same bed, both of us trying to think of something to say, something that would reach across this open space and keep us together. Keep us a family. So we usually said nothing, and neither of us was sleeping very well. But you're something different. I used to wonder if you wanted to talk, and then I was afraid you were thinking really deep, important thoughts and I didn't want to disturb your concentration while you were trying to save some tribe from genocide or something."

"And now you know I was just thinking about your ass in a flight suit."

IT WAS nearly morning when the sounds of weeping came through the wall from the garage. John sat up, threw his legs over the side of the bed, and Gabriel sat up with him. "John, is that Kim? It doesn't sound like him."

"Let's find out." He pulled on his sweats, and Gabriel slipped on a pair of pajama bottoms and a tee shirt. John knocked quietly on the kitchen door to the garage, then pushed the door open. Kim was sitting on the side of the bed with another boy. There was a strong smell of beer and cigarette smoke in the air, and the bed was covered with the pieces of Kim's big cameras, the professional models. The boy was weeping, his face turned to Kim's shoulder, and Kim had an arm wrapped around him, was talking in a soft little singsong voice, like he'd use to soothe a scared child. The boy looked up when John and Gabriel walked in. "It's okay," Kim said, and it sounded like he'd said it a thousand times already. "You're safe here. This is my Uncle John and my Uncle Gabriel. They won't hurt you, I promise."

The boy was small and frail, and looked impossibly young. He had a little blue streak in his fair hair. John had seen him walking into Effex with Brain Walker the night they had gone with Kim. The boy's pretty young face was purple and bleeding. Someone had pounded him viciously with their fists. His mouth was cut and swollen, and the left eye was purple and closed shut, with a laceration through the eyebrow that had three neat stitches. Blood was spattered down the front of his white shirt. "You've been to the ER?"

"Urgent Care," Kim said. "The ER's too expensive. Billy only has the university's health insurance."

John reached behind him and pulled up a chair. Gabriel had disappeared back into the kitchen, came back with a glass of water. "You have any pain medicine? Tylenol?"

"I think I've got some in the bathroom," Kim said.

"I'll go look." Gabriel handed the boy the water, and he took a thirsty sip. He came back with a bottle, shook a couple of capsules out into Billy's hand.

John studied them. "Kim, you have a clean tee shirt Billy can sleep in?"

Kim looked around the room like he'd never seen it before. John could see the strain on Kim's face. Both of the boys looked close to breaking down. Billy had just started to wail first.

"Okay, hang tight." John went into his bedroom, pulled out an army tee shirt and exercise shorts, and brought them back to Kim's room. He handed them over, went into the bathroom, and looked for a clean towel in the linen closet. "Okay, Billy, you get in the shower and get cleaned up, then lay down on Kim's bed. I'm going to bring you a little ice pack when you're asleep for your face, to keep the swelling down."

"Kim, can you stay?" Billy was shaking when he tried to stand, like his legs wouldn't hold him, and he reached out and clutched Kim's arm for a moment.

"I'll stay." Kim waited until Billy was steadier on his feet, then went to his outside door, checked the lock, and checked the windows. "Okay, everything's secure. I'll just be in the kitchen with my uncles while you're in the shower. I'll leave the door open, Billy. You'll be able to see us. Okay?"

Billy nodded, went into the bathroom, but left the door half-open. Kim followed John into the kitchen, propped his bedroom door open with a kitchen chair. "Billy, I'm right here."

Kim sat down at the table. John studied his shattered face, pulled out the folder from the PI about Brian Walker from his briefcase. He opened it to the photos, pushed them across the table to Kim. "These are the boys who had to get medical care after dating your professor. The PI I hired got access to their records. These photos were taken at the hospitals. You see the dates, Kim? The first was taken four years ago. A long time before you were ever on his radar. A long time before I was. This isn't about you or me. This is what he does."

"I'm having a hard time accepting that right now—that what happened with me didn't lead in some way to this. Violence leads to more violence, everybody knows that."

"Kim, that's such a simplistic way of looking at things, too simplistic. You don't understand, son. Motivations and the conflicts that arise between people are so much more complicated than it seems on the surface. You can't explain the mysteries of human behavior with a phrase you can print on a tee shirt."

Kim gave a hiccup of a laugh that turned into a cry, and he covered his face with his hands. Gabriel picked him up, sat down in the chair, and cradled him in his lap. Kim curled into Gabriel's chest, cried like his heart was breaking. Maybe it was. "Kim, you've got to trust us. Trust your Uncle John. I've seen him pull off miracles. I've seen him negotiate peace between tribes that were armed with enough old Russian artillery to wipe out a couple of mountains, with a hundred years of violence between them. It's about trust, okay? He didn't explain what he was doing then. He didn't need to. We trusted him, trusted he had a plan. And in over twenty-five years, Kim, he never betrayed his code. He never behaved unethically to get a job done. Once you take the high road, you don't change your mind and decide halfway up the road's too hard, too rocky, or too steep. You don't turn around and take the easy way. We're taking the high road because it's the right thing to do. We didn't call in the black ops guys to take care of this bastard. We're doing this the right way, working through the system. You have to stand tall and trust us to see this through."

Kim laughed, a shaky, bitter little sound. "I swear, do you hear yourself when you talk? I have to trust you, because you didn't even consider letting me handle this my way, and now it's out of my hands, a snowball of retaliation, gaining velocity. About to reach critical mass. We sound like some stupid gangster movie. 'He sends one of yours to the hospital, you send one of his to the morgue.'"

John actually thought that was a reasonable blueprint for the current situation.

"That was a good movie," Gabriel said, and John grinned at him across the table. "Sean Connery, really hot."

Kim raised his eyebrows in disbelief. "Sean Connery's hot? If you say so." His eyes were cool when he looked across the table at John. "I want to be very clear about this. I don't believe you when you say this has nothing to do with you and me. But I will handle this situation from here out. You do not have a dog in this fight. Billy is my friend and he came to me for help. I would appreciate it if you would not approach Brian about what happened tonight."

John leaned back in the chair, studied Kim. "I will not approach Brian, agreed. That would be counterproductive at this point. But don't tell me what I can or cannot do, Kim. What I'm trying to accomplish, the negotiations that have already begun? You do not have a dog in *that* fight, my friend. And hell will freeze over before you dictate terms to me." They stared at each other across the table, and John was pleased to see the strength in Kim's face, despite the tears, despite his position curled up on Gabriel's lap. "You want to let Billy stay out in the garage with you? If it gets to be too much we can put him up on the couch. I'll be home tomorrow, so I can look after him. You tell him so he won't be scared when he hears me."

Kim's eyes brimmed with tears again, and he launched himself forward into John's arms. "I knew I could bring him here. I never doubted for a minute I could bring him and you would help me. Not everybody would be willing, you know? That nurse at Urgent Care called the police. She made Billy get pictures taken. He tried to tell her no but she just rolled over him."

"Good. That's what she was supposed to do. He wouldn't talk to the police?"

"Kim? Are you there?" Billy's voice from the bathroom was tremulous, shaking as much as his knees probably were.

"I'm coming, Billy."

CHAPTER 9

JOHN CLOSED the kitchen door after Kim, and Gabriel started working on the Mr. Coffee. John went back to his office and pulled out a legal pad and a pen, then joined Gabriel at the table. "Let's get started." He looked up, noticed the grin on Gabriel's face. "What?"

"'You don't have a dog in this fight.' Is that kid for real?"

"He's learning how to be a man, stand up for what he believes. Stand up for his friends. I'm happy to see it, actually." He tapped the pen against the paper for a few moments. "Not every boy has to reject his father to become his own person, despite what the ancient Greek playwrights suggest. I hope Kim and I can coexist with our divergent world viewpoints for many years in the future. Until he comes around to see that I am right." He grinned at Gabriel now. "Or until I come to see that his way is right."

"I'm looking forward to seeing that. You must be doing some calculations again, your eyes are like stainless steel." He hesitated, then got up and poured two mugs of coffee. "John, how old is that boy? Shit, when he walked into the bar the other night, I thought he didn't look any older than Juan, and I should have followed up and made sure he was safe."

"I saw him too, and had the same thought. I'll see if I can find out. But I agree. Even discounting the issue of the violent assault, he seems too young by about a hundred years to be running with the likes of Brian Walker."

"I have access to some software that should let me find out the basics. I think we can do that much without causing Kim too much grief."

"I want you to do something for me today, if you would. Contact Dean Fox, let him know that my resignation, while it was in response to the issue under discussion, is not a bargaining point."

"You've decided to move on."

John was struck for the moment at Gabriel's choice of words. "It's just a job, Horse-Lord. I'm not ever going to move on from you. Not unless you tell me to get lost. And then I'll probably just moon around Albuquerque, drinking my lunch and taking naps and remembering the glory days, and your ass in a flight suit."

Gabriel was staring down at his cup. "I don't want to cling around your neck so hard we both go down. But it's good, right? I mean, it's good being with you. Just like regular guys, not secret lovers. If we'd had this problem, like suddenly we had nothing to say, and the awkward silences started getting longer and longer... oh, man, that would suck."

"It's good." He reached across the table and took Gabriel's hand, let their fingers slide together. "Better than I ever imagined, having someone to talk to. I feel like a regular little chatterbox."

"You haven't spent any time with my daughter, have you? Speaking of regular little chatterboxes." His hand tightened on John's. "If anyone ever touches her like that bastard touched Kim, or that poor boy in there, I will come after him with every weapon at my disposal." He took a deep breath. "Even if my baby tells me I don't have a dog in that fight."

John laughed, but he felt his throat close up for a moment, thinking of the fear in Billy's eyes, the way he'd cringed back when they'd opened the door. "What I am used to doing is keeping a squadron safe. The dynamics are different in a group when you have leaders who can watch out for their people. How do we keep them safe when they roam around town on their own, go into bars, eat at Ho Ho's, go to classes with professors who like to hit them? With no platoon leaders to keep an eye out?"

"Is it too late to send them all to Catholic school? I mean, the Jesuits have some universities, right?"

"But back to the point, I have decided to move on from teaching leadership seminars and freshman civics. What I have to say will need to be said a different way."

"You've always written."

"I enjoy the company of scholars, though I have noticed the use of intellectual discussion as a means to forestall action much too often in that group. It's a hard nut to swallow, making a decision and moving forward, knowing you might be wrong. When the stakes are very high. But I've learned to swallow that nut. Most of the time, it's not fatal to be wrong. Maybe 65 percent of the time, on a bad day. Those aren't bad odds."

"So, leadership?" Gabriel winced. "John, you do realize, in the civilian world, leadership means politics?"

GABRIEL LEFT for the office, his jeans and tee shirt folded on the chair in John's bedroom. John wrapped an arm around his waist before he left, took a little bite out of the caramel-sweet skin on his neck. "Come back here tonight." He thought about saying, *come back tonight, don't leave me alone with these two hurt boys*. But it wouldn't have been true. He could use Gabriel's help, no question, but he'd really just wanted him again. Wanted him in his bed, again. Wanted the smell of his shampoo in the bathroom. Wanted to see how neatly he tucked his dirty socks into the laundry bin. John shook his head. Give him a little bite of something sweet, suddenly he was starving for more.

Kim left for Ho Ho's at about ten thirty, said he had class, not with the crazy professor, at two, and he'd try to be home after if he could get someone to cover the dinner shift. Billy had agreed to sleep in, and he would open the door to the garage when he was awake. John understood by the stern look Kim gave him that his role was to provide lunch and clean towels and no questions.

Chicken noodle and grilled cheese was the go-to lunch for hurt boys and upset stomachs and broken hearts in the general's house. He'd eaten little else when Gabriel had told him he intended to get married, six weeks at least, until he shook it off and told himself he needed to grow up and get real and get back to work. Gabriel had loved him so hard back then, like he was storing it up for a lifetime of loneliness, and John really thought he'd never see him naked again. They'd lasted about a month after the wedding before Gabriel had leaned against his office door, asked him if he'd like to go to the O Club and get a steak, and his face had been so humble and hurt, such an ache in his dark eyes, that John had pulled him into his office and closed the door behind them.

It was noon, and John could hear Billy moving around in the garage. He didn't open the door, though. When John heard the muffled weeping again, like a boy would sound when he pressed his hurt face into a pillow, he went to the door and knocked. Billy opened it a moment later, holding a towel up to cover the battered side. "I bet you need a new ice pack. And I've got lunch ready. You should probably eat something before you take more pain medicine on an empty stomach."

Billy let himself be herded to the table, ate his chicken noodle and grilled cheese, and took the two Tylenol the general put in his palm. "Are you in the graduate art program with Kim, Billy?"

The boy shook his head. "I'm still an undergraduate. In art, though, mixed media and printmaking. I thought New Mexico would be cool, you know? It's got a reputation as being supportive of artists."

"Where are you from, originally?"

"Cheyenne. Wyoming." This was said with a gloomy look at the table. "It's going to be harder than I thought it would be, to find a place to fit in. A place where I can be myself."

"It is for everyone, Billy."

"Not for you. I mean, it must have been easy for you, you're...." Billy stopped, obviously thinking back to the two men who'd come in to check on him in the night.

"I went into the army after college. That was the place I fit in best. I was very happy there, with the work and with the company. Military people, they tend to be warrior-philosophers. Deep thinkers, strong, able to act when need be, with stainless-steel balls. Most of us can leap tall buildings with a single bound, or, I should say, we've been known to try." This last got a laugh from Billy, as he'd intended.

"Kim told me he'd never been afraid when he was in your company. He always knew you were strong enough to protect him."

"You can be assured that protection now extends to you too, kiddo. As long as you're under my roof, no one will hurt you."

"Thanks for letting me stay."

"You're welcome."

The knock on the front door startled Billy so much, he jumped up from the table, tears pooling in his eyes. John stood very close to him, but didn't touch him. He could see the new bruises around his wrist, along his forearm. "Let's go into the garage, okay? You'll be safe there. I'll knock on the door when it's safe to come out."

"How will I know it's you?"

"Shave and a haircut, two bits."

"Huh?"

The knock on the front door came again. "Go on now, Billy." John went to the door, opened it to Dean Fox.

"General! Can I come in? I hope I'm not interrupting your lunch."

"Not at all. What can I do for you?"

"I heard from your counsel this morning, Gabriel Sanchez. He's retired army, isn't he?"

"He is."

"He has that military bearing. Also has a no bullshit way of getting down to business."

"That's a way I appreciate as well."

"So I'll get down to it." Dean Fox gave him a wry smile. "You certainly keep the kettle on full boil, General. The president tells me under no circumstances should I let you resign. Your admin, Cynthia,

96

comes to me with her hand over her mouth, little squeaks of distress, and says you run a violent office. Professor Walker comes in and tells me to rein you in before he calls in some favors and has you whacked. Just kidding about getting you whacked."

"So which of these issues brings you here today, Dean Fox?"

"Please, call me George. Cynthia, of course. A good admin is hard to find."

"I agree. Let me go get my little tape recorder, okay?"

"Oh, God, I was afraid of that. You always have such excellent documentation."

"I grew up during Watergate."

John came back with the recorder that fit in the palm of his hand. He played back the conversation between he and Brian Walker in his office, and when he got to the part where Walker made his comment about Kim bending over like a little Korean dog, Dean Fox blanched, held a hand out to stop him. "You sure you don't want to hear the rest? There is about to be the violence Cynthia was forced to witness."

Dean Fox shook his head. "I just don't...."

John stood over him for a moment. "Dean, will you excuse me for a moment?"

John knocked on the garage door. Billy opened it to the secret knock. "So that's what that knock means! I never knew."

"Dean Fox is here to see me about another matter. You know him? He's the dean of students."

Billy nodded, and John could see a cringe. "Son, you need to stand up right now and go in there and talk to him. I'll go with you." John put his hand on Billy's shoulder. "Stand up like a man, and get this job done. You know it's the right thing to do. You aren't the first, but maybe you can be the last."

"He won't tell the police, will he?"

"You tell him the terms, Billy. But he should know what his professors are doing. You're a student at his university. This happened on his watch. Give him a chance to do the right thing."

"I don't know what you're talking about half the time," Billy said. "You sound like one of those Cheyenne cowboys I grew up with. I never knew what they were talking about, either. Some secret man code."

"Your daddy a cowboy?"

"Yeah. If he knew about this, he'd…. Oh, God, I can't even imagine."

Billy walked into the living room ahead of John, and Dean Fox came to his feet when he saw him. He looked up at John, his face sick, and John moved Billy to a chair, stood next to him. Dean Fox sat back down on the couch like his knees couldn't hold him.

"I'm Billy Dial."

"Hi, Billy. I'm Dean Fox. We've never met before."

"I saw you, though, at new student orientation."

"You're a student here? What year?"

"I'm a freshman in studio arts."

A freshman? John's head came up at that, and he stared at the Dean until Fox lifted his eyes and met his.

"Billy? What happened? Somebody hit you."

"It was Professor Walker. Brian Walker. He was… we were dating, you know."

BILLY LAY down on Kim's bed after the dean left, and John pulled up a straight chair, sat next to the bed reading a book until the boy fell asleep. A freshman. Eighteen? Seventeen? He wanted more than anything to pull out the phone directory and call Cheyenne, Wyoming, and bring a little cowboy justice down on Brian Walker's ass.

He'd need to have that conversation very carefully with Billy and Kim. Kim called about four to report he couldn't get anyone to cover his shift at Ho Ho's, so he'd have to work. John told him he'd stay at home with Billy, and handed the phone over to Billy when he was done.

"We'll talk when I get home, okay?" Kim sounded rushed and a little overwhelmed when he got the phone back, so John assumed Billy had told him about talking to Dean Fox. After Billy fell asleep, John propped the door to the garage open and sent Gabriel an email, telling him what had happened. Gabriel emailed back about an hour later, saying he'd be home by six, and Martha had given them a tentative okay to the tutoring.

John loved the way that sounded: *I'll be home by six*. He had spent more of his adult life than he could have imagined, when he was eighteen and a freshman in college, listening to the echoes of his footsteps walking down the hall of an empty house, to sleep alone in an empty bed.

CHAPTER 10

HE HAD chili ingredients, and everyone liked chili, so he cooked a pot for dinner. Billy helped him chop up green chilies and onions, and John noticed he'd painted his fingernails a very delicate pale pink to make himself feel better. "I used Kim's nail polish. You don't think he'll mind?"

John shook his head. It was news to him that Kim had nail polish. What was he using it on, his toes? John had never seen any polish in evidence. It occurred to him, for the first time, that Kim had possibly made adjustments to his behavior in order to live in peace with his uncle. If so, he'd been very quiet about it, and this was something new for Kim. New and mature, John thought, feeling quite pleased.

Gabriel came home and put his briefcase on the kitchen table, wrapped an arm around John's waist and nuzzled the back of his neck. "Chili smells good."

Billy watched them out of the corner of his good eye. John remembered what Kim had told him, about wanting to have had a role model, to see someone be in a real relationship as a gay man. He reached a hand up to Gabriel's cheek. "Hi, handsome. Welcome home." He thought it probably sounded even more lame than it felt, but Gabriel looked surprised and pleased and Billy giggled a little behind his hand.

"I brought some potting soil for the cold frame," Gabriel said. "I didn't get seeds, though. It's your project."

"You can get the seeds. My initial burst of enthusiasm with woodwork was in response to not having a job. I was over it in about seven hours."

Gabriel leaned over and smelled the chili. "How about herbs, then? Basil and rosemary and lemon thyme?"

"Okay with me."

"Is the wonder boy coming home for supper?"

"He's got the dinner shift at Ho Ho's."

"I'm going back to the dorm," Billy announced, surprising them both. "I feel better. I mean, I can't hide out here, and I know Kim didn't get any sleep last night. I'll drive by Ho Ho's and tell him thanks, and that I'm okay."

"What am I going to do with all this chili?" John wasn't sure this was a good idea.

"You can freeze it into individual portions," Billy said, looking very serious and helpful.

"Oh, okay. Thanks, Billy."

Billy held out his hand, and John shook it, saw a glimmer of tears in his one good eye. Gabriel leaned back against the cabinet. "Billy, you sure you can drive with one good eye?"

"I came on my bike. And I live in those dorms down off Amherst, so I'm really close."

John reached for the legal pad on the table, wrote down his cell and email. "I'm your emergency contact, okay?"

"John, give him my office number, too. Never know when you might need a lawyer to ride to the rescue."

Billy nodded his thanks, stuffed the paper down into his jeans pocket. Then he reached out, gave John a hug around the waist, and was out the door.

John pulled open his phone and called Kim. "Yo! Uncle J, what's up?"

"Yo to you too. I wanted to tell you Billy just left for home on his bike. He said he was okay, and he looked better."

"Okay." John could tell Kim was chewing on his thoughts. "He told me earlier he would go home tonight if he felt better. How did he look to you?"

"He put nail polish on."

"That's a good sign, in case you didn't know."

"I figured it out. Later, son."

Gabriel pulled open the fridge and grabbed a couple of beers. He twisted off the tops and handed one to John, leaned back in his kitchen chair. "You're a good guy," he said. "You take care of everybody. Your squadrons and your tribes and your kids. I don't see you taking care of yourself very often."

John turned from the stove, surprised. "What do you mean? I have everything I need."

"No, you don't. You have one enormous crater in your life. A sinkhole. What you need, that you don't have? Love. A relationship. Me. In your life. Permanently."

John was speechless. What was he talking about? "You've been in my life for most of my adulthood, Gabriel."

"On the down-low. That's not what I'm talking about."

John pulled out a chair, sat down next to him, and took a long pull on his beer. "Gabriel, okay. So what are you talking about? You're still married, remember? I mean, it's not like we can just…."

Gabriel put his beer down, a line of bad temper going down between his brows. "Oh, yes, we can. You're saying I'm jumping the gun. Why can't we talk about you and me?"

"So let's talk. Have I given you any reason to think I'm not interested?"

Gabriel shook his head, staring down at the floor. "Sorry. I'm tired. Tired and frustrated and I want to know you've got my back. I don't want to be out in the world alone, dangling at the long, lonely end of a piece of string. I'm not trying to put you on the spot."

"You can put me on the spot. Why don't you move in with me? Were you waiting for me to ask you? I didn't want to complicate things. I mean, your life seems a bit complicated right now, doesn't it? But if I could have anything in the world I wanted, it would be you, in my bed every night. At the table with me every morning. Living with me. Spending your life with me. I think if you do, it will upset Martha and may cost you in your divorce. I guess that's what I was thinking, that the legal stuff is still pending. But I've already got your tools in my shed. I can't think of anything I want on this earth more than knowing you're going to wake up in my bed every morning. I want this. You, I mean. I want you. Is that enough for now?"

John thought he looked tired and a little scared. "Yeah, it is. More than enough. And I'm sorry. I wasn't trying to push you into anything. Or maybe I was. John, did you see those boys at the bar the other night? They weren't just out and proud, they were out and proud in flashing neon, you know? I'll never be that far out of the closet. I'll never be anyone but myself. But it seems to me I've been missing something critical. I see that in you too. Missing the right to love. The right to make a life together. We shouldn't have had to give that up. And I feel the loss, like there's a hole in my chest, a wound. Sometimes it feels like my heart looks like that poor boy's face looks—beat all to hell. It pisses me off that we've lost all this time. And I don't want to wait any longer."

John studied his face, a mixture of bad temper and yearning. "Okay. But I made chili for supper. Can we eat first?"

Gabriel started grinning, the tension flowing out of his shoulders, and he laughed and got up and opened the cabinet doors, pulled out a couple of soup bowls. "I love chili. Did you put beer in it?"

"You know it, brother."

"I'm forty-eight, John. I mean, shit, my dick could give out any time."

"I'm fifty-two. Mine will probably give out first. Not that I've seen any evidence of that so far."

"It's just a matter of blood flow. Right?"

103

John shrugged, biting down on his bottom lip to keep from laughing. "Yeah? So?"

"I have a plan. To get the blood moving."

"Super Freak" - Rick James

"Addicted to Love" - Robert Palmer

"La Bamba" - Los Lobos

"Shakedown" - Bob Seger

"Walk Like an Egyptian" - The Bangles

"'SUPER FREAK'? Gabriel…"

"It's my eighties get-the-blood-moving playlist. What's even better, I've got the music videos so we can have visual cues in case we've forgotten how to dance like an Egyptian." He moved into a pose, a perfect hieroglyph. "Just try it one time." He was laughing under his breath, and he took *Battleship* out of the DVD player. "You're gonna love it."

John stared at him. What a week. What a crazy fucking week. Maybe they needed some "Super Freak." He kicked off his shoes, pulled off the socks so he could dance barefoot. "Okay, hang on while I put these in the laundry."

When he got back to the living room, Gabriel had loosened his tie, another long and thin black one. Didn't Robert Palmer, in the video…? He was still wearing his work clothes, but John didn't say anything. Clearly this was part of Gabriel's dance routine.

"You do this every day after work?"

Gabriel shook his head. "I can't every day. Sometimes I go out into the garage for some private dance time. Anything to keep from going mad."

John couldn't help but laugh at Rick James in his wig, covered in glitter, and Gabriel swinging his ass to the music. It was impossible not to dance to "Super Freak," and he was singing and swinging before they were a minute into the song. He couldn't believe it, he remembered all the words! Had he heard the song that many times on the radio in 1981? Screw it, he could sing if he wanted in his own house! He grabbed a wooden spoon off the countertop to use as a microphone. Gabriel was executing some nifty spins, and John leaned over backward with his spoon until he looked like he was playing limbo. They both sang into the microphone for the last *she's super freeeeekaay.*

Gabriel grabbed him for a little dirty dancing when Robert Palmer started, and John could feel that the blood was moving without any trouble, their hips flowing together to those great rhythms, and then Gabriel spun away, moved his hand up to that skinny black tie. *Might as well face it, you're addicted to love.* John used his wooden spoon to good effect, enjoyed the show when Gabriel managed to dance his way out of his tie and dress shirt.

Gabriel took his hand when "La Bamba" came on. Lou Diamond Phillips looked so young on the screen, just a baby, really. John let Gabriel lead them through a little flaming salsa. They both lost their tee shirts, then their pants, which was a good thing because when Bob Seger took the stage, they needed to be dancing skin to skin to boxer shorts. John remembered dancing to this song once before, an entire squadron a long way from home on Christmas Eve, and Bob Seger had gotten them all over their blues. Everyone had danced together, from the youngest soldier to the general, while a dust storm raged outside the hanger. Their DJ for the night had taken the microphone, said, "Let's shake it down for all those pretty babies waiting for us at home, in Minneapolis and Pensacola and Memphis and my home town, Flagstaff, Arizona!" John had danced to "Shakedown" with a young soldier who worked in the chow hall. He still remembered the shock in that kid's brown eyes, and the silly grin on his face when he'd found himself dancing with the general.

Gabriel reached to the coffee table when the song ended, retrieved the wooden-spoon microphone and handed it over. "You're gonna need that. Now watch an expert walk like an Egyptian, my friend," he said when the Bangles took the stage. John could tell Gabriel had danced to this song many, many times since 1987. He *was* an expert!

"Oh, my God! Look at the hair!" Kim had wandered in from the garage. He didn't seem to notice the two uncles walking like Egyptians in their boxers across the living room. He was staring at the Bangles on the TV screen with their pink guitars and tambourines and big eighties hair. "Look at that, she's got a lace catsuit! I've got to get one of those."

A lace catsuit? John and Gabriel looked at each other and watched Kim go back to the garage and close the door. Now John believed the nail polish was Kim's. What else he had out in that garage, John didn't want to know. Gabriel pulled John close. They were both breathing hard from the dancing, and John felt the rocking of their chests, skin to skin, hearts beating so close, just a couple of layers of muscle and bone between them. Gabriel leaned over, kissed his ear sweetly. "I've got the *Ultimate Barry White Collection* in the CD player next to the bed." He wiggled his eyebrows up and down, and John laughed and thought, *Yeah, I would say the blood's moving.*

CHAPTER 11

JOHN WATCHED Gabriel sleeping. He sprawled out, half on his side and half on his stomach, one hand hanging over the side of the bed. His skin was so warm and brown, his silky hair the gorgeous color of Russian sable, not quite brown and not quite black. John pushed the hair back from his face. He'd always loved the feel of it, fine and delicate. Gabriel still had plenty of hair. Forty-eight, and when he was asleep, he looked twenty-five. Maybe some lines next to his eyes, but they just looked like he'd been smiling.

John pulled on a pair of sweats and went into the kitchen to make breakfast. He had something to look forward to, an article for Monocle on leadership among the ancient Greeks. People never seemed to get enough of Sparta and Athens, fighting against the devilish Persians. It would be a fun article to write. He'd not read his Xenophon for some time.

He pulled open the fridge and stared inside. Something special, a little treat for Gabriel. They could eat bacon, just this once, without worrying about the cholesterol.

The house smelled like heaven, coffee and bacon and English muffins toasting. Gabriel came into the kitchen, his face damp and freshly shaved, his pale-blue dress shirt tucked into navy trousers. He looked happy, John thought. Gabriel sat down at the kitchen table and

John brought him a cup of coffee, and Gabriel took his hand, said, "Thanks."

The simple pleasures were the ones that brought the most joy, John thought, looking down at Gabriel's head when he bent over the coffee cup. This was a memory they should have had from a hundred mornings, but it was new, something bright and beautiful: a handsome man, his lover, drinking coffee at the kitchen table after they'd loved each other the night before, and slept the sleep of happy men.

Gabriel looked a question up at him, and John put his hands on his face, looked down into his dark eyes. "I love you. I haven't said that before, have I? I hope you never doubted it." John leaned over and kissed him, tasted the coffee on his tongue, smelled the bright citrus scent of his aftershave. Gabriel reached for him, slid an arm around him, and John could tell he was smiling. He tasted like hope and happiness, like the possibility of every morning for the rest of their lives. "I love you, and I made you bacon for breakfast."

"I know," Gabriel said. "About the love and the bacon."

JOHN WORKED on his article most of the day. He had an email from Gabriel, asking him to come to Ho Ho's for some afternoon soup so they could talk about the tutoring with Juan. Martha wanted to talk to him. He gave Billy a call, woke him up, but Billy sounded okay, said he was going to check in with Kim later.

When he walked into Ho Ho's, there was a sleeping homeless guy in the back booth again. John thought it was a different guy from the last time, but he couldn't be sure. There was a tableful of coeds, and they were eating, talking, and texting on their phones, all at the same time. Juan was sitting at a table with his mother. John stared at the back of her head, and Martha turned around and looked at him. She put her hand on a chair and pushed it toward him, an unmistakable invitation.

He sat down, nodded to Juan, who studied the tabletop.

"I thought, since you might be spending more time in the future with my children, we should get to know each other a little better."

What? "I'm always happy to see you, Martha. Juan, how are you?"

"I'm okay. Do we have to start on the algebra today? Kim could probably use some help bussing tables."

"Yes. But fifteen minutes should be enough to start."

Martha raised her index finger. "I would like to sit in, if I may."

"Sure, of course." He turned to Juan. "Did you bring a notebook?" Juan nodded, pushed the notebook toward John. "We're just going to talk about a few basic principles today," he said. "Algebra is all about relationships. It's about writing out mathematically how things are related."

Martie came bouncing out of the bathroom, hopping like a little kangaroo. She looked like Martha, but with Gabriel's silky hair. It was long, nearly to her waist, pulled back in a ponytail. John could see wispy curls along her neckline. She was wearing a navy-blue pleated skirt and a white polo shirt, neatly tucked into the waistband. John remembered what Gabriel had said about Catholic school. She leaned against the table. "Is this him?" She looked at Martha, and Martha nodded at her, gave her a stern face, and put a finger against her lips.

"So let's start by talking about two...."

"So you've been dating my dad for, like, over twenty-five years? Even before he met my mom? That means you're homosexual, right? Because you're not married. But my dad, he's bisexual, because he had me." Martie pointed to her chest. "I made a note on my Facebook wall that my dad was bisexual. Lots of my friends think that's cool. I got fourteen likes. There's a girl at school, her name's Amalie, she has two mothers who are lesbians. We talk about nontraditional families because Jesus loves everyone, no matter what they do. Are you and my dad going to get married? I think that would be cool. I could be the flower girl in the ceremony. Or if you just wanted to do a commitment ceremony with rings, I could still be a flower girl, just not with a white dress. Like, maybe a flowered dress."

Kim brought over a pot of tea, laid a hand on John's shoulder in silent support. Martha looked furious, furious and heartbroken, and John was reminded this new nontraditional family that was so cool to her daughter was not what she had signed up for. Martha looked up when Gabriel walked in the door, and then she looked at John, eyes narrowed, looked to see what was in his face when he looked at her husband. While he was sitting at a table with her children. John thought if she'd had a shiv in her hand, she would have shoved it into his heart.

"So one way of thinking about algebra is to remember that some things change and some things don't. We distinguish between these things by calling them variables when they can change, and constants when they don't change."

Juan dropped his head to the table. He refused to look at his father. "Seems to me everything changes."

Martie had flung herself into Gabriel's arms, and he was holding her up, her legs wrapped around his waist, listening with growing dismay to her plans for his commitment ceremony. Her voice was pitched too high, a frantic little sound, words falling over each other, and there was a line of damp along her forehead. Gabriel was rubbing her back, trying to quiet her, saying, "Daddy's here. Hush now, baby. Daddy's here."

It occurred to John for the first time that this was going to hurt. That he had something to do with what was happening, that he had some responsibility for these people. That his role was more than just a supportive friend and lover, while Gabriel changed his life. John could see very clearly for the first time that he was a part of what was happening, and it was not going to be easy, not for any of them.

GABRIEL TOOK the kids out to supper so Martha could have a few hours to herself. John hoped she was using the time to take a nap or have a couple of margaritas and talk about what assholes men were with her girlfriends, rather than looking for a hit man.

John was reminded how cool Gabriel was, how smart and how strong, when he came in from dinner with the kids, gave John a smooch, and got his briefcase out and started working at the kitchen table. John was working at his desk on the article for *Monocle*, and the house was peaceful. The quiet felt like bliss. Kim stuck his head in about ten, said he and Billy were working on an art project out in the garage, so if the uncles heard noises, they should ignore them.

John was happy to ignore any noise from the garage, but he stuck his head through the door to see how Billy's face looked. He couldn't tell, though, because Billy was working on a mask, a black mask that covered the damaged half of his face. He looked like a petite, fey Phantom of the Opera. He seemed pleased when John told him this. "Listen, Billy, when you went to the Urgent Care the night you got hurt, did they ask you about next of kin? The name of the person who was going to pay the bill? Anything like that?"

Billy nodded. "I know I'm going to have to call my dad. If he gets a bill from Urgent Care and I haven't told him about it, then he's really going to be upset. I've been avoiding it, actually. I mean, I've got three older brothers, General Mitchel. I don't want them to make me go home." He took off the mask, drew around the eye with a tiny tube of glue, and sprinkled it with glitter. The swelling was worse, but none of the abrasions looked infected. "I'm thinking about going home, but I want to decide myself, you know? I don't want to get rescued and carted off to Wyoming, proving their point that I'm not safe without all three of my brothers standing over me, ready to kick the ass of anyone who insults me." He looked up with a sad little grin, then slipped the mask back on. "Especially now I've had my ass kicked, I take the threat a lot more seriously."

"Dean Fox might call him too. I just want you to be ready."

"Did he seem worried to you about liability? Or was he genuinely concerned?"

"Maybe 20 percent concerned about liability. The rest was real and all concern for you, Billy."

"That's about what I thought. He seemed really nice."

"Enough chitchat! Out, out! We're creating here!" Kim was shooing him out the door.

"That door locks both ways, kiddo."

"Oh ho! The uncles want some private time! You don't have to tell me twice."

John shook his head, went back through the garage door. That kid was a piece of work. What was he up to now?

Gabriel was yawning, picking up the files, and putting them back into his briefcase. "I've done nothing but sit on my ass all day. So why do I feel so whipped?"

"You want to run with me in the morning? I've got a three-mile loop. Just enough to keep the knees from getting stiff."

"I'll run with you." Gabriel went back into the bedroom, dug around in the overnight bag he'd brought yesterday. He pulled out a tee shirt and a clean pair of socks.

John caught him around the waist. "Why don't you bring everything? Bring it all, okay? Just bring everything, and we'll deal with the fallout."

Gabriel wrapped his arms around him, rocked him a little bit. "You sure? You know it won't be easy. I'm not pushing you into this, am I?"

"I'm sure." And he was. John watched Gabriel getting undressed, sitting on the side of the bed to pull off his socks, and he remembered him when he was a hotshot young pilot, wings so new they were practically damp, remembered the eagerness in his touch. Remembered the shyness and the question in his eyes, the first time they'd touched like lovers. Gabriel had always followed his lead.

But John wondered, watching him ease back, his head on the pillow, sighing when he stretched his back and started rolling around, finding his position to sleep, if Gabriel hadn't always wanted more. Maybe he had always hoped for something more, right from the very beginning. If so, then John thought that logically, what they were all going through right now was a consequence of his failure. Had he had a failure of leadership himself? The thought had never crossed his mind before. What if he'd said, way back when he'd realized the feeling between them was deep and strong and real, what if he'd said right then, let's take a chance. Let's risk it all. What we have, you and me together, it's worth more than anything. What would Gabriel have done? He'd have come into John's arms, nodded his head yes, and followed him anywhere. Their lives would have been different, but for the first time, John wondered if he might have made a mistake, and chosen the wrong path.

In the middle of the night, John felt Gabriel's hand reaching for him, cupping his face, stroking the angle of his jaw with his thumb. Gabriel moved his hand down across John's chest, down to his belly. He slid his fingers into the wiry hair in his groin, then wrapped his fingers around John's cock. "There you are." Gabriel's voice was sleepy, and John thought he was smiling. "Just making sure it's you. It's so wild, isn't it? Me and you, every night...."

Gabriel curled around in the bed, and John felt his warm breath against his thigh, then Gabriel's soft mouth touching him. His belly was tight, his cock swelling at the unexpected touch, yearning sinking down through his skin, heat and sweetness, lust and love lodging against his spine, deep in a place only Gabriel could reach. Then Gabriel was climbing up his body, pressing him against the mattress. He held John down, hands on his wrists, took a bite out of his neck. Gabriel was hungry, thrusting his hips, and John felt their cocks slide roughly against each other. "John, can we...?" He could hear the longing in Gabriel's voice, feel the desire in the roughness of his hands. John rocked against him, let Gabriel thrust hard, and then he lifted his hips, wrapped his legs high around Gabriel's waist.

Gabriel groaned, his mouth moving down John's neck, and John reached down between them, wrapped Gabriel's cock in his fist. "Anything," John said, and Gabriel lifted himself up, looked down at John, hands on either side of his face, pressing down into the pillow. Gabriel's pupils were huge and black, his eyes as wild and dark as a desert sky full of stars. "Anything you want."

Gabriel looked down at him and smiled, then bent close and let his mouth touch John's. "Roll over," he said.

CHAPTER 12

JOHN FIXED a pot of coffee, and they both drank a cup while warming up out on the driveway. The morning was still cool, but the crystal blue sky and the smell of spring flowers told him it was going to be hot before ten. Gabriel was looking up as well, with something like lost hope on his face. "Good day to fly. Would you look at that sky?"

John thought about Gabriel without a chopper. Hard to imagine, but he had a house, a family, two kids in Catholic school, Juan in braces, and he'd only been working as a lawyer for less than a year. He'd picked a strange little group practice that seemed to spend too much time helping people get their immigration status fixed, and defending boys with HIV when no one would rent them an apartment. He still wasn't making what his salary had been when he retired from the army, and didn't seem to think he would anytime soon. He probably didn't need the extra expense of a newly divorced father's studio apartment. But John didn't want to push him too much. He'd offered. He'd give him a couple of days to think about it, and they could talk again.

They finished the three-mile loop, an easy, flat run perfect for aging knees, and were walking up the street to the house when a car pulled up next to them. Dean Fox rolled down the window and stuck his head out. "General? You have a minute?"

"Sure. You want to come up to the house?"

115

He shook his head. "I just knocked on your front door and Kim chewed my ear off for ten minutes. That boy's scary first thing in the morning."

You have no idea. "So what can I do for you?"

"I wanted to give you a heads-up. I don't think there will be any comeback, but I'm giving Brian Walker his resignation letter today. Billy Dial, hey, do you know who his father is?" John shook his head. "Cody Dial. He's a bull rider, world champion for six years running back in, what was it, '92 to '98? Something like that." Fox shoved an elbow out the car window. "Man, he was more popular than Jesus where I came from. Anyway, I got a call from him last night, no idea how he got my number, and he's on his way from Cheyenne to look after young Billy. I guess Billy called him about thirty seconds before he called me. You don't have any idea where Billy is, do you?"

John shook his head again, and Gabriel spoke up. "Dean? Could I suggest you give Brian Walker the letter before his father has a chance to stick him in rehab? Because once he does that, he's got a medical condition, and that's going to complicate a termination for cause. I think he probably does have a problem with alcohol, maybe something else, but do you want him back on your faculty? Around students? What's going on with that guy, it's more serious than just substance abuse."

"I didn't think about rehab. He does need something to fix whatever is wrong with him, no question. His department head, he should have told me things were getting this far out of control."

John stared at him, and Fox looked a little shamefaced. "I guess it didn't seem as real to me as it did with Billy sitting in front of me, so young. He's just a kid, so vulnerable, and he was here at my school, and one of the professors? I just can't bear it, John. Once I get Walker off the faculty and take care of Billy's father, I'm sending in my resignation as well."

John was surprised.

"I know you blame me for not acting sooner, John, and you would be right. I blame myself. The president would never go against me on this, and he didn't when we had a private talk yesterday. Too many old bones in both our closets, you know what I mean? I read that article you wrote for *Civil War Magazine*, about the failure of leadership among the northern generals. It really said something to me, John. The only thing I can do at this point is try and get back on the right path."

John saw he was looking at Gabriel over his shoulder, and he couldn't remember if he'd ever introduced them. "George, have you met Gabriel Sanchez? He's my counsel." John looked back at Gabriel's handsome dark face, watched him lift his arm and wipe sweat from his forehead. "And my partner."

"Your partner in what?" Gabriel slung his arm around John's shoulder, and John watched the dean's eyes get big with comprehension. "Oh, right, right, sorry. It's been a rough couple of days. I'm slow on the uptake. That's right, the army, they've got that 'Don't Ask, Don't Tell' thing, right? Oh, wait, they stopped that. Now they say it's okay?"

He was babbling, and John stopped him before it got any worse. "Thank you for coming to let me know about Professor Walker. Does Billy know his dad is on the way from Wyoming?"

"I don't know. I tried to call him but no one answered his phone."

"I'll speak with you later, then." John turned back toward the house. He knew George Fox was watching them in the rearview mirror, probably drifting across the yellow line, and he didn't want to be responsible for an accident. Gabriel was laughing, though, reached out and pulled John into his arms and kissed him, a deep sweaty soul kiss right on the streets of Albuquerque, at 0748 in the morning. "You never called me your partner before, not in all these years. You've never said it out loud. You've never told anyone."

John leaned against him for a moment, resting his face against Gabriel's strong brown neck, and closed his eyes. He smelled so deliriously male. "It's way past time, don't you think? That I claimed you for my own? I should have done it years ago. In the light, the way you wanted."

Gabriel was shaking his head. "It's easy to look back and second-guess. It's easy, on a day when the gay boys are so free to be themselves, and join the gay student club, and look on the internet to find the gay bars in any city in America, to forget what it was like just a few short years ago. We did the best we could, John. All we have to work with is today."

"And today I love you, and you're my partner, if you want to be. How does that song go? 'You're all I've ever needed. Baby, you're the one'."

"Are you quoting Elton John to me? Now I know you must be gay." Gabriel ducked out of the way when John tried to swat him. "I've always been yours. I tried hard to make it work with Martha, John, I really did. I gave it everything I could. But you were there first. In my heart, I mean. You've always been the one in my heart."

They walked into the house, arms around each other, and Gabriel went off to the shower. Kim must have been watching for the very second he could have John for himself, because he burst into the kitchen like a little fireball to tell John everything Dean Fox had said. But he ended up just telling John what he had said to Dean Fox, since the man had not been able to get a word in after Kim started in on him regarding abusive men lurking among the faculty.

"So why do you suppose that you got so riled up over Billy, when you wanted to hide your own face when he did it to you?"

"He hurt Billy a lot more than he hurt me. And Billy's young, he's just eighteen, and…."

"Billy isn't a child. He's smart and tougher than you think. So why?"

"Why what?" Kim was cruising the fridge. "Do we have any bacon?"

"What happened to the Buddhism? Never mind, don't tell me. You just think about it, okay? Why you're treating Billy differently than you treated yourself. Add it into the mix, for whatever you're plotting down at Ho Ho's."

"Did you ask the Horse-Lord to move in? Juan said that his mom said that it was only a matter of time, and she didn't know why he bothered with the fiction of his own apartment."

John sighed. He wondered why they didn't just ask Martha what they should be doing. She had a real clear eye when it came to the general and her husband. "Can I remind you again that you aren't a spy gathering information from the enemy camp, and Juan is young and angry and hurt, and he needs a friend?"

Kim smirked at him. "*Juan* is angry and needs a friend? I feel like patting Mrs. Horse-Lord down for weapons every time she comes in. Actually, you're right, she's very smart, and Juan tells me she paints, she has a little art studio out behind the house. I might get her to help on the—" He hesitated. "—on the Ho Ho's project."

John pulled out the English muffins and wondered why Kim couldn't just stick his fingers into the business of the multitude of friends that flocked around him like bright little birds. There always seemed to be a crisis going on with that bunch. But maybe this was Kim's business. This was affecting both of their families. "What do you think about all of this?"

"What do I think? I think it's long past time you and the Horse-Lord were together like you should have been all along. I think it just shines out of you, when the two of you are together. The love, I mean. On both of you. Oh, that reminds me. I want to take some pictures of the two of you like saints. You know, the Virgin de Guadalupe. Or Bernadette. Yeah, Bernadette. I think that look on your face when you're together, it's the same look on the saint's faces, when they're having visions. Very camp. Like somewhere between a vision quest and a psychotic break."

John stared at him, tried to let the disbelief shine out of his face. "Out. I'm trying to cook. And tell Billy to come in. I need to speak with him."

Kim saluted him, his back ramrod straight. "Aye, aye, General."

Billy stuck his head in the kitchen door, looked around like he was scouting for enemies.

"Good morning, Billy. Do you want some eggs for breakfast?"

Billy shuddered and pushed his hands away. "Oh, God, no. I can't take food this early."

"Then how about some coffee?"

119

He shook his head. "Do you have any herbal tea?"

John opened the cabinet over his head. "Kim has some tea bags that say blood orange, hibiscus, and rose hips on the label."

"Oh, perfect!"

John tossed him the tea bag, pointed toward the electric kettle and the mugs. He waited while the water heated and Billy poured hot water over the little tea bag and put a saucer on top of the mug. "The key," he said, "is steeping properly so it develops a rich flavor. This tea has more antioxidants than you probably get in a month eating a normal American diet."

"Really?" John waited for more.

Billy leaned back against the countertop, tried to look casual. "So I decided to call my dad last night. I told him not to come, that I was fine and I'd be home for spring break, but my guess is he's on his way."

John handed over Kim's bottle of unfiltered raw honey and a spoon. "Dean Fox came by this morning. He told me your dad's on the way."

"Kim told me George was here, but he didn't have much to say." Billy studied the wall, waiting for his tea to steep; then he sighed and opened the jar of honey, put a big, dripping spoonful into the mug.

The general waited again.

"He didn't say anything about my brothers coming, did he?"

John shook his head.

"The thing is, when I'm back in my room at the dorm? Everybody is staring at me and asking questions and frankly, they all seemed pretty thrilled at the drama of it all. I don't appreciate being the week's entertainment. I don't like being a poor little victim. That is so totally *not* me. But I don't want to put you in a bad position by staying with Kim. Like, when my dad comes bursting in here with guns blazing."

"Would you like me to call your dad and tell him who I am, and that you're staying here?"

120

Billy took a big swallow of the tea. "That's what I was hoping, General Mitchel, but I don't want you to be uncomfortable. I know you and your lover are just moving in together, and that's always a hard adjustment for everyone. I don't want to make anything more difficult for you."

John bit his lip to keep from grinning. There was more to young Billy than was evident at first look. He was smart enough to know when to tell the truth. "Gabriel and I have been friends for a long time, Billy. We're cool. Don't worry about that. You are very welcome here. Let me have your dad's cell phone if you want me to call him, and I'll give him directions to the house. Can you tell me, is he uncomfortable with you being gay? Is he likely to give Kim any reason to give him a lecture on civil rights? We should prepare if that's the case."

"Wow, you really do think like a general!" Billy drained his tea. "No, sometimes he looks like he's in pain when he talks about it, like he's got a stomachache, and I get the feeling he is trying really, really hard to not say anything to hurt my feelings, but what he thinks about it in the privacy of his own bathroom, I don't know. I know he believes in a strong united front against all opposition."

"So do I. We'll get along fine."

JOHN DECIDED to tackle Gabriel at dinner and force a discussion of the elephant in the room. One of the elephants. He'd cleaned out his closet earlier, put all but two good suits in the closet in the office, and cleared some drawer space for Gabriel's clothes. He cleaned out space in the bathroom, one drawer and one shelf, in what could only be an invitation to move in. Only one more thing was left, and it was critical.

John locked the door to the garage, in case Kim decided to spring in on them with his camera and saintly drapes. He fired up the grill, cooked a couple of sirloins just the way they liked them. Gabriel was putting butter on his baked potato. He was so handsome, John thought. He moved with a grace and power that was almost startling. His face in profile looked like something classical and Greek. It wasn't just that he enjoyed Gabriel's company. He was smart and strong, and so gorgeous

121

John felt sweat break out along his hairline, down his back. But there was still something more, something unique and wonderful that was all him. "Do we need to talk about the kids?"

Gabriel looked up, his eyes narrowing. "What about the kids? Mine or yours?"

"Yours. I wondered if you felt comfortable having them here. If you were living here, with me, would you want your kids here? For visitation? For summer break so Martha could go on a cruise?"

Gabriel sat back, stared at the wall, and John cut into his steak. Pepper, he'd forgotten the pepper. He went to the cabinet and brought back the grinder. "You want some?"

Gabriel nodded, then leaned over his plate and cut a piece of steak. "Yes. To everything."

"Good. So, how do you want to do it? I was thinking we could move a second desk into the office so we could both have work space. That would leave one bedroom we could make up for the kids, or we could bunk Juan out with Kim in the garage and leave the bedroom for Martie."

"Did you hear what she's calling us? Double Dads. That's the name kids have for a pair of dads. She's put on her Facebook wall that she has a bisexual father and now she's got Double Dads!! She wanted a picture of us but I said no. Martha is so very pissed off. She's stuck raising them every day, and we get the fun weekends and the cute nicknames. John, are you sure? Sure about all of this? I mean, you asked your old boyfriend to bunk with you during the divorce. My life seems to be more complicated than I anticipated. Do you really want all of this?"

"I didn't ask my old boyfriend to bunk here during the divorce. I asked you to move in with me. You, the person I've loved forever. I assumed that meant the kids too, but I figured we might want to let Martha ease into it a little. Gabriel, I never asked before. I wonder now if that was a mistake. But I will tell you frankly that it no more occurred to me we could ever live together, like lovers, than we could live together on the moon. It just… never occurred to me."

"I used to imagine it. I thought we could find some small tropical island and go there to live. But then I would think about two weeks in. What would we do all day after securing shelter and clean water? Would there be tribes who needed a mediator? Could I devise some sort of coconut-powered flying machine?" He shook his head. "This is the world we live in. We just needed to be patient and wait for it to catch up with us."

"It was a long wait, Gabriel. For some generations of men, they waited forever. It's hard for me to think about them now, what it must have been like. They were really out there alone. But I did wonder about something else. We might as well talk about it now. You've never had a chance to play the field. You're moving from one house into another, without being single, without the fun of being single. Sure you don't want to play with the boys and girls a little bit? After all, according to your daughter's Facebook wall, you *are* bisexual."

"This? Me and you? This is as wild and crazy as I'm likely to get, unless I'm in a helicopter. Then all bets are off."

Gabriel worked on his steak for a while, and John did the same. The kitchen was filled with blissful silence.

Gabriel put down his fork. "Let's see what Kim thinks about letting Juan bunk with him. Otherwise Juan and Martie'll be fighting in the middle of the night and we'll have to put masking tape down the middle of the bedroom floor."

John nodded. "Sounds good. Maybe Martha could let them spend a day. Martie will want to decorate her own room, I suspect."

Gabriel pushed his empty plate back. "Count on it. You know the thing that scares me most of all? That she would marry some creep just to annoy me. And that guy would be living in the same house with my kids. He could fuck with Juan's head, and do God knows what to Martie."

"It could happen," John agreed. "She could get married again."

"She will," Gabriel promised. "Just to prove that she's still beautiful and desirable. I don't think she'll ever put the kids at risk. But smart women have been fooled before by creeps."

"We'll be sure to carefully vet anybody that looks to be getting close. The kids will tell us what's going on."

"I've got a question for you. You're changing too, and it's not just me. Letting me in, I mean. You used to be really structured. You kept things compartmentalized, you know? And now you're open to things. Open to change, and me. I mean, do you know what you did today? You said in public we were gay. Did you mean to do that? Are you going to come all the way out of the closet, become Retired Army General John Mitchel, the gay silver fox?"

That surprised a laugh out of him. "The what?" He shook his head. "I don't know, Gabriel. I think it's you. Your love is working on me in mysterious ways."

Gabriel reached across the table and took his hand. "Thanks for the space in the closet. And the bathroom. Thanks for opening your heart to me and my kids."

"You're welcome."

"I'll bring the rest of my gear after work tomorrow."

"Okay. And by the way? We're expecting company. The cowboys are about to land."

CHAPTER 13

BILLY'S FATHER, the retired bull-riding champion Cody Dial, sounded tired and impatient on his cell when John introduced himself. "Are you the Army General John Mitchel?" The sound of the wind, and the road, was loud, and John thought he had the window of his pickup truck rolled down.

"Yes. Retired."

"That's what Billy told me, but he has been known to exaggerate in the past. I looked you up. Strategy and Tactics for the Joint Chiefs. How about that. You've got a Wiki page."

"So do you. He's not exaggerating about the beating. What did he tell you?"

"Some jerk he was dating had too much to drink and popped him one. He had to get stitches in his eyebrow."

"It's more serious than that, but we can discuss what's being done when you arrive. I just wanted to give you a head's up. He was hurt badly, mostly to his face. He had some bruising on his ribs too, and some marks on his arms and wrists. I don't know what else. He's... a little afraid."

John listened to the sounds of breathing over the phone.

"Is the motherfucker who touched my son locked up?"

"Not yet."

125

"That's good," Cody said. "Then I'll take care of him myself."

"Come see me first and I'll tell you what's being done. Billy's staying in the garage with my nephew Kim."

"Are they boyfriend and girlfriend? Or whatever you call it?"

"Not that I know of. I think just friends," John said. "Kim was hit a few weeks ago by the same man, who is one of their instructors."

"This sounds like there's more to this fucking story than I am going to like. I'm nearly in Durango. I'll be there in six hours."

IT WAS past midnight, and Gabriel was asleep. John had stayed up to keep the light on for Billy's dad. Cody Dial was a man of few words. He shook hands, said his name, then, "I'd like to see my son."

Billy Dial must have had a beautiful and petite mother, because his father was a plug-ugly beast, with a face like a potato and a nose broken more times than it had been set. The look on his face when he stared down at his youngest son, asleep in Kim's bed, his pretty young face purple and swollen and cut, was nearly too painful to see, and John turned away to give him some privacy. He sat down on the side of the bed, and Billy stirred, woke up, and went into his big father's arms. John stepped back into the kitchen, put on a pot of coffee.

He sat with Billy for more than fifteen minutes, until John heard him murmuring, "Go to sleep now, Billy. Daddy's here. You go on back to sleep." He came into the kitchen a few minutes later, took off his ball cap, and ran both hands back over his hair.

"You want some coffee? Or I have herbal tea."

"I only drink that herbal tea when Billy catches me at a weak moment. I'll take a cup of coffee."

He pulled out a chair at the table and sat down, and John poured him a cup and joined him at the table. They looked at each other for a long moment, and John was pleased with what he saw in Cody Dial's eyes. He looked smart and in control. "I've got some papers to show you, and a report from a PI." Cody nodded, and John went to his desk and got a file folder. He'd prepared a copy of all the materials he'd gathered for Billy's dad.

Cody studied the papers, drank his coffee, and when he finished, he had two questions. "When I was in there talking to Billy, Kim said, 'This is all my fault.' Kim thinks what happened to Billy was some sort of revenge. What did you do to this guy after he hit Kim, other than what is in this paperwork?"

"Called him out in public. Punched him in the knee. Torn ACL. Not a great deal of permanent damage, but I hope it hurts like a bitch."

"Kim, he doesn't realize a guy like this doesn't need to go looking for a reason."

John was happy Cody Dial realized that as well.

"You think his father has been protecting him, keeping him on the faculty?" John nodded. "And what you're trying to do is get him off the faculty and his father out of a position of authority, correct? And you're working through the system to accomplish this?" John nodded again. "I believe you and I work on different sides of a line, General. A spoiled, rich man who has been protected by his daddy when he hurts young men who are his students? I don't know if a man like that has any incentive to reevaluate his behavior. What's his motivation to change?"

John looked at him carefully. "I would hate to see a man like this responsible for ruining any more lives. He tries to poison the people he touches. Our boys, they're both strong and smart. They're working on their own model for this. For healing, I guess you could say. I'm working on this my way. That may be enough."

"No offence, General, but my experience has been that some men don't change unless they have a reason to change. Revenge is a sucker's game. That's not what I'm about. But I will make sure my son will not ever be touched again by this motherfucking piece of dog shit. That's all you need to know about it."

"You want a bed? I can make up the couch."

"I thought I would just sit with Billy."

"You've been driving a long time to get here. He's just in the next room. Might as well sleep."

"Maybe I will. Thank you for your hospitality, General Mitchel. How long you been out of the army?"

"I retired a year ago."

"How did you make the adjustment?"

"It's been a little rough. I wasn't expecting all the changes, to tell you the truth."

"Life will surprise you."

CODY DIAL was up early, and John got to see the look on his face when he introduced Gabriel. It took a moment before Billy's father realized they were more than overage roommates. It did look to John like a slight stomachache. Cody just sighed, though, and shook hands and said he was pleased to meet him. He said things were changing faster than he could keep up with. Then he pulled out his phone and called Dean Fox. "George Fox? This is Cody Dial. I'm on my way to see you." John could hear squawks coming from the phone. "It's only six? I must have come from a different time zone. Well, you better get on up, or you can open the door in your pajamas when I knock."

Cody closed his phone and stuck it into the back pocket of his Wranglers. "That's funny. He didn't seem all that pleased to hear from me."

"He told me yesterday morning he was going to find Brian Walker and fire him. If that is not what happened, would you mind giving me a call?"

"Sure, General. What do you have in mind?"

"I need to go see the cabinet minister for education up in Santa Fe. He asked me to come teach at the university when I retired, and I need to explain to him why I left. Also, I want to get a face to face with Brian Walker's father. His name is Prentiss Walker, and I need to get a feel for the man before I plan the next step."

Gabriel put his cup of coffee down. "I also think you should both consider using the media. We've got that hot-dog investigative reporter downtown, Charlie Green, and you know he would splash word of a cover-up at the university and on the board of supervisors all over hell and back. That would bring about a change, no question. And that's what we're going for, right? A change in the current way of doing business?"

"Yes," John agreed. "But. You know he would want to talk to the boys and none of them have agreed to this. Seems to me unlikely they would agree. I don't want them hounded or made to play the victim."

"Something to consider, we could invite him to whatever Kim is planning at Ho Ho's. I think it would be worth thinking about, because this isn't a private affair. It's affecting our families more than most, but this community supports the university. It depends on the university being run with an eye to the safety and education of the children. I don't see that happening, and the community has a stake in seeing things change."

"He sounds just like a politician, don't he? You're a good talker, boy." Cody Dial put his ball cap back on, winked at Gabriel, and went into the kitchen to peek through the door into the garage, where Billy was sleeping.

"Good God." Gabriel said after Cody Dial left, rolling his shoulders. Looked to John like he was getting ready for battle. "I wonder if we're ever going to see Brian Walker in one piece again? Okay, forget I said that. What have you got on your plate today?"

"I need to proof the article for *Monocle* and send it in."

"I told Juan I would take him up in the chopper this afternoon after school. He agreed to work harder on the algebra."

"You want me to have another go with the tutoring?"

"You up for it? We could meet at Ho Ho's after we take a spin. Kim offered to take a picture of the two of us. Juan said, 'Yeah, great, we can call it a picture of me and my dad, the year he ruined my life.'"

"Maybe I'm not the best person to do this."

"I don't know, John. I don't seem to have any idea what he needs me to do. I can't quite get my mind around not knowing what to do. I mean, he was always my little shadow, you know? He's been glued to my leg since he could crawl. I don't want to think this is going to change things between us for good. But it might. I didn't really think how it was gonna look to him. I wanted a quiet divorce. I never thought Martha would throw this in my face, make it public. I should have lied when she asked me, but you always said lying backfires, and I wouldn't have felt right about it. About denying what was going on."

"You mean, make you and me public? To the kids?"

He nodded. "I wasn't quite ready for that. I didn't know what to say, and it wasn't just my privacy at issue. I didn't say anything to Martha that would make her assume I was leaving her for you. I mean, I wasn't. It wasn't like that. I was leaving because I couldn't... I couldn't lie anymore about my heart." Gabriel grinned, a little sadly. "About the nature of the beast. Martha decided the kids ought to know, because she knew it would hurt me to see them upset. And it did. So now Juan's fourteen and trying to get his mind around the idea his dad's gay. Kim he's cool with. I mean, Kim is wild and flamboyant and colorful, and Juan has always looked up to him, so anything he wants to do is cool. But he was not expecting me to be gay and he doesn't like it and he's secretly wondering if this might be hereditary. He's known you his whole life, and now you are not the person he thought you were, either. Just like me."

"Adults are not supposed to change like this, out of the blue. I'm sorry it happened this way. But Gabriel, I'm not sure there's anything we can do about it now."

"We shouldn't have had to pretend our whole lives. Always on the down-low. Always watching our backs. We can't get that time back, John. You know I loved the army like I love the air I breathe, but, Jesus, what a cost. If we had been honest from the very beginning...."

"If we had, you wouldn't have had the kids at all."

Gabriel stood up, pulled John into his arms. "No, you're right. You're right. They make it all okay. Maybe it cost us twenty-five years, but they are irreplaceable. Don't you think? And you and me? We have plenty of time."

JOHN WORKED on the article in the quiet of his office and wondered what was happening. No one called him, though, so he suspected things had not reached a crisis point. Either that, or he had become entirely inconsequential to everyone. Kim and Billy went off to class, and Gabriel went to work. He enjoyed the writing, wondered if this solitary and quiet occupation was going to be the one he finished his life with. It was hard to imagine, after being one of the favorite thinkers and problems solvers for the JCS. But times changed. He felt like what he needed to do most was help Gabriel through this next year. Work on the two of them becoming a couple, becoming a family, rather than just two independent men who loved on the down-low.

He walked over to the third bedroom, looked inside. He had some exercise gear and file boxes stored against the far wall. They would be easy to move to the shed. Hard to imagine the walls painted lavender, with little rainbow ponies or whatever Martie might be interested in. He thought she was probably into ponies. Maybe unicorns.

He had the bedroom cleared and his article proofed and emailed to the magazine by early afternoon. He wandered outside, saw that Gabriel had put potting soil into little pots in the cold frame. He couldn't tell if there were any seeds, though. Kim called and saved him from himself. "Yo, I'm on my way to get you! What are you wearing?"

"Clothes."

"Make sure you look good. I'm taking a picture of the Horse-Lord in his flight suit."

That was the most interesting bit of news John had heard all day. "Just honk when you get here."

He looked down at himself. Jeans and a chambray shirt that was faded to a soft color between blue and gray, just the color of his eyes. Maybe this would be his retirement uniform. He ran a hand over his chin and his tongue over his teeth. He'd do.

Kim studied him with dismay when he got into the car. "What is this new look? You're like an unemployed Mr. Greenjeans. You haven't been messing around with the cold frame, have you? We already planted the seeds."

"Where's Billy?"

"I haven't seen him since I dropped him off for class. I think he's going to meet up with his dad later. He said he didn't think his dad was up for Ho Ho's, so I don't know if I'll see him tonight. I told him he had a bed for as long as he needed one, but I think Mr. Dial is probably going to haul him off to the Holiday Inn until he can convince him to go home. That's my theory." Kim drummed his fingers against the steering wheel. "Why don't you let me take a picture of you and the Horse-Lord together?"

"Why?"

"Because that's what couples do. Real art photography, it says something more than the simple subject of the picture. I want to see if the two of you are… I don't know how to say it. Melding." Kim lifted his hands from the steering wheel and showed what he meant. John thought it looked like he was pulling saltwater taffy. "It's part of your coming out. Photographs of the lovers together, that's one of the things men of your generation missed."

"If I agree to this, will you stop talking?"

"Probably not," Kim said, with what John thought was a particularly inane grin, "but I'll try."

When they got to the airfield, Gabriel was head down in the cockpit and Juan was sitting cross-legged on the tarmac, playing a Nintendo, his back to the chopper. Gabriel looked tired, but the flight suit brought back so many happy memories that John went into his arms and kissed him. Gabriel looked pleased, kept an arm around John's shoulders while he showed him the chopper. He had a painting on the nose of a great silver-white warhorse with big black eyes, and he told the story of Torii Motoada, the samurai who died to protect his lord. Juan rolled his eyes, unimpressed. Kim was working the camera, taking some snaps of the two of them together, and Gabriel pulled John back against him, bent over, and kissed him on the neck. He looked over at Juan, then looked away. "You want to fly with me? I'm about ready to blow this pop stand."

John turned into him, wrapped his arms around Gabriel's waist. "Yeah, I'll go with you. Anytime." He looked at the little helicopter. It was an MD-500, and looked like a plastic toy next to the Apache attack helo Gabriel had always flown.

Gabriel smiled then, and Kim said, "Hey, Uncle John! Look at me for a mo, okay?" When John looked at him, Kim took the photo, then smiled at them over the top of his camera. "Yeah, I got it. I am so frigging good, it's scary. Hey, Juan, come to Ho Ho's with me? I'll drive real fast, and we can leave these two old guys in the dust."

Gabriel kept his arms around John's shoulders. John looked up at him. "You want to go? Fire that pony up."

"Don't tempt me. I might just keep going. We'd be like the gay, retired army version of Thelma and Louise, in a helicopter." His face was a mix of sorrow and mad that John had never seen before. "That little shit said he didn't want to fly with me!"

The phone rang in John's pocket. The caller ID said Cody Dial.

CHAPTER 14

FATHER AND son Dial agreed to meet at Ho Ho's. "I heard some interesting things today, General. I thought I might pass them on to you. Then I'm going to pack up my boy and take him home."

"Did you see Brian Walker?"

"See, that's one of those interesting things. Seems he's disappeared. Had a leave of absence approved by the president without the dean's knowledge, and he's taking a little mental health break in some unknown locale."

"I see." John felt the mad creeping up his neck. "I'll speak to you soon."

Gabriel was staring at him, eyes narrowed. "Uh, oh. What's happened? The general looks like he's doing some calculations."

"Wainright bought our boy a ticket out of town before Fox got a chance to fire him. Prentiss Walker must own a big chunk of his ass."

Ho Ho's looked even more seedy and depressed than usual, the windows and serving counters smudged and greasy. The women behind the glass counter were having some dispute in Vietnamese whenever they passed each other, their faces stiff. Kim was uncharacteristically silent, head down over his wok, and young Juan was wiping down tables and not looking at anyone. He was wearing a sticker on his apron that said *volunteer*.

Cody Dial looked slowly around the restaurant, and then he pulled up a chair. "What the hell kind of name is Ho Ho's? You think it's somebody's idea of a joke?"

John shook his head. "Sometimes ideas don't translate well." Kim brought a large teapot and a pile of little cups. John took them from his hands, passed them around.

Billy looked even smaller today, his face darkening to the color of an ugly thunderstorm. He seemed on the verge of weeping. Cody kept a hand on the back of his chair.

"So the professor has split town, destination unknown. I was in George Fox's office today. Wainright was there, and they got into a screaming fight half the university must have heard. Fox resigned, threw his resignation letter in Wainright's face, and Wainright said something like 'that son of a bitch Mitchel, I am going to screw that little army prick into the ground.' I got the feeling he was talking about you, General." Cody was showing his teeth in a ferocious little grin. John felt himself doing the same.

Gabriel pulled out a memo pad and started making notes. "John, we need to move quickly. You two decide right now, media or no?"

John and Cody looked at each other, and then at Billy. He was staring down at the table, his bottom lip caught between his teeth. They both shook their heads no.

"Then we need to go to Santa Fe in the morning."

"Dad, we can't go home yet. Please, just until me and Kim have our art show, okay?" It was Billy, speaking up for the first time.

"What is this art show?"

"We're doing a special art show here at Ho Ho's. Please, it's really important. Dad, it's important to me. It's only a week. We can stay that long, can't we? Then I'll go home with you."

For the first time, Cody Dial seemed a little unsure. He looked at John and Gabriel, but Billy tugged on his sleeve. "Dad, this is how me and Kim want to handle things. Why don't you listen to us? This has something to do with us, you know? And we feel like we know how to make things right. I think all of you ought to give us a chance."

"Okay, son. A week, then home before your mother has a conniption fit."

Gabriel was shaking his head, and John reached out, put his hand on Gabriel's arm. "Let's go home. We've got some work to do." He stood up, offered Cody Dial his hand. "I'll call on you if I may."

"Yes, sir. Anytime."

Juan stared at them from across the restaurant, and Gabriel walked over to talk to him, but Juan turned away, started wiping down tables he'd already cleaned. Gabriel's jaw was tight when he walked out of the restaurant. He shook his head. "What in the hell is going on with that kid?" He shoved his hands in his pockets. "We got no time for that now. We need to be in touch with Lathrop tonight. Have you talked to him?"

"I emailed him a copy of the report a week ago. My guess is he's asked Wainright for an explanation, a *what the fuck is going on* sort of explanation."

"Good. So what's Lathrop been doing in the last week?"

"I got the feeling he was looking for ammunition to give to the governor, so she can put a burr under Prentiss Walker's ass. They want to use this to get him off the board of supervisors, that's fine with me. But he's not going to go easy. It would be helpful if we could figure out what his comeback is going to be. Other than hiding his son. There's some power struggle going on between the governor's office and the board. They're going to use this issue as a weapon in some larger war."

"That's for the politicos in Santa Fe. We've got to stick with the single issue that concerns us, then get the hell out."

"Agreed."

"Where do you think Brian Walker's hiding?"

"Not far enough away from Cody Dial. I have the feeling that man will hunt him down until the end of his days, if that's what it takes. So that means we can concentrate on Prentiss Walker. And when we're done with him, we can concentrate on me and you."

Gabriel looked at him in surprise. "Me and you?"

"Me and you. Kids and ex-wife. Our wonderful life. The life we should have had together, and the one we're going to live from here on out. You think Martie would like lavender walls in her room? And maybe little unicorns?"

GABRIEL STARTED researching properties owned by Prentiss Walker, thinking there was a little cabin somewhere and Brian Walker was holed up like some idiot outlaw. John went for a long walk. He always did his best thinking while he was walking, and he needed to think through what the opposition was doing. Charlie Lathrop, up in Santa Fe, had received a copy of the report a week ago, sent John a quick email saying he would be in touch. Prentiss Walker had had a copy about the same length of time, from Wainright. What would Walker Senior's major concern be? Maybe not protecting his son's reputation any longer, but trying to figure out what the hell was wrong with him and was he about to go to jail. Pressure on Brian Walker was escalating since John had called him out in Effex, and that snowball was rolling down the hill. Daddy Walker had probably come to Albuquerque to see him, or sent someone, and after that, young Billy had been attacked.

The kids at Effex had seen the banner, had taken pics of it with their little cell phones, had talked about what was happening on Twitter and Facebook. Billy had gone to Urgent Care, and like it or not, reporting agencies had gotten involved. Pictures had been taken and the police had been called. At that point, Prentiss Walker's motives must have changed. Now he was in retreat, and he needed to get his son out of the reach of the law. But that's not all he would have done. A good general always had a flanking movement to distract the enemy. A nasty little mosquito to make the enemy look away when he needed to concentrate. What would Prentiss Walker do to distract him? He needed to go see the man, take his measure. Then maybe he could outthink him and stop an attack before it occurred.

He would go for Kim, or Gabriel. Who knew what Kim had been up to? If there was a person on the planet less likely to be blackmailed, John couldn't imagine who that might be. Kim would love to get blackmailed. He would splash his indiscretions across the smudged front window of Ho Ho's. Gabriel? Gabriel had a very angry soon-to-be ex-wife and a son who was acting up, and his daughter had just announced her new Double Dads on her Facebook wall. Was Martha planning something and Juan knew about it? Maybe his recent behavior was because he was being torn between loyalty to his mom and his dad. But what could she do? And what did it have to do with Prentiss Walker? Martha was smart, too smart to be manipulated easily. But she was so angry. Sometimes anger like that could blind you.

Walker was about fifteen years older than John. His generation, they didn't like to be embarrassed in public. They weren't part of the digital age, where every detail of your current status was updated routinely for the world to see. Maybe what he was planning to do was publicly out the general and the Horse-Lord. And he was going to use Martha to do it.

John looked into the office. Gabriel was studying the computer screen, wearing a pair of reading glasses that made him look incredibly sexy. Everything made him look sexy. John shook his head. So what was new? Gabriel was just....

"I'm going out for an hour or so. Pulling on a thread."

"You have an idea?"

John shook his head. "Not sure yet. Let me see what I can come up with."

Gabriel sat back, pulled off his glasses. "Do I get a kiss before you go?"

John pushed him back in the chair, kissed his neck, up his throat, along the angle of his jaw until he made his slow way to a warm and smiling mouth, the softest mouth, always open, always smiling.

He grabbed his briefcase and walked out to the driveway before he called Martha to say he was coming over. "We need to speak privately."

"Is Gabriel coming?"

"No. Just me."

SHE WAS watching for him, and came out to the driveway when he pulled in. She opened the passenger door and got in the front seat of his car. "We can talk out here." She was wearing sweats, her dark hair pulled back in a ponytail at the nape of her neck.

He turned off the car, and they listened to the silence and the tick of the engine cooling. She still looked tired, but defiant too. "Martha, I need to explain to you about the current situation."

"Like I don't know the current situation?"

"I'm not talking about our personal business. I'm talking about Professor Brian Walker being physically abusive to his students. Including Kim." She looked up at that, startled, and he handed her a copy of the folder that held all the information he'd gathered. He watched her go through the pages carefully. At the back, John had put in a copy of a photo Kim had taken of his face with the black eye and swollen, cut lip. He'd drawn big arrows with a magic marker, pointing to the purple swelling under his eye, and written along the bottom "Help! I'm turning into a blueberry!" She smiled at this picture, let her fingers reach out to touch his face. She'd known Kim since he was a baby too.

"Why are you showing me these?"

"I need to know if Brian Walker's father, Prentiss Walker, is going to try and use you to derail me. I'm trying to get this man off the faculty. His father is a member of the board of supervisors and is protecting his son. Protecting him to the point that he is letting him continue the abusive behavior. He knows I'm working on this. Have you been approached by anyone in the past week, two weeks? Someone from the media?"

"If I have been, it wasn't anything to do with this."

John let silence fill the car. "You have talked to a reporter about our private family situation?"

"Excuse me, General, situation? It was my family, not yours. It's not a private family situation. It's adultery. It's you and Gabriel, lying

140

to me, cheating on me, for the entire length of our marriage. You can pretend it's just a little family matter, but the UCMJ would have said something different. If you had told the truth, if anyone had found out what you two were doing, you would have been kicked out of the army. You could have been court-martialed for adultery. And the Uniform Code of Military Justice still applies to you. They can still court-martial you for things you did while you were on active duty. They can still throw you into Leavenworth. They can strip your rank and your retirement benefits."

John felt the chill fill his belly. "Martha, what have you done? Who told you all this?"

"It wasn't a reporter. It was a lawyer. He took a deposition about what I know about your relationship with my husband. He said he was going to forward a copy to the inspector general."

"And the purpose of this deposition?"

"I don't know. I hope he uses it to burn your life to the ground. Like you've burned mine."

John looked at her for a long time. He remembered the fortune cookie he'd opened at Ho Ho's. *And where the offence is, let the great axe fall.* He'd assumed at the time Hamlet was talking about someone else. "Martha, I'm sorry for what's happened. I'm sorry you've been hurt, and the kids. I've loved him all my life. Nothing you could have done would have changed that. Nothing you do now is going to change what's between us. He's like the air I breathe, you understand? But I am sorry for hurting you, more than you could know."

She got out of the car, handed the folder back in to him. "And I'm sorry about what happened to Kim and the other boys. That doesn't have anything to do with me. If your man is behind the lawyer approaching mine about the deposition, then I would say it's just too damn bad you left so much ammunition lying around for an enemy to use against you."

GABRIEL WAS out in the yard when he got home. John saw the bottle of tequila and the pitcher of orange juice on the counter, along with

Gabriel's phone. John fixed himself a glass and joined him in the yard. He was looking down into the cold frame.

"Early days yet, isn't it? For seeds to come up?"

"Yes, it is. I'm thinking about getting a little thermometer, though, so we can monitor the temperature." He stood up, took a big slug of his drink. "She called me as soon as you left. You didn't tell me you were going to talk to her."

"It was just a hunch. And I wanted to make sure things were okay between us. In case she had some things to say to me privately."

"So what do you think now?"

"Things are not okay between us." They walked to the back porch, pulled a couple of chairs over, and sat down in the dark. John could feel the chill air rising from the ground. "Gabriel, would they do it? Would they lay charges and proceed with a court martial?"

He shook his head, then hesitated. "Not about homosexuality. Not since DADT has been abolished. It would be… no. Impossible. But they've always looked with a hard eye at adultery. That's how they used to go after men when they wanted them gone but didn't want to publicly name them as gay, or embezzlers, or criminals of other flavors."

John flinched a little, to hear "gay" set in the same sentence with "embezzler." He remembered, though, and it felt familiar to him, familiar from living under that fear for most of his life. And now he was mad and scared, mad at the army and Martha and the fools who filled up the world, lived their lives without ever thinking about the consequences. "Fucking hell. What about the security clearance? Being homosexual was always considered a security risk, because people would become susceptible to blackmail. The work I did in the last tour, for the JCS. Is that going to come into question?"

Gabriel was shaking his head again, but John felt the ice still sitting in his gut, some slight tremor in his chest. They could take it all from him, everything. And the thing that meant the most to him, the work he had given his life for, his reputation. Maybe the inspector general wouldn't want to do anything in public, but his colleagues? A lifetime's work could be called into question because he had kept it hidden, and that had made him a blackmail risk. He'd never have received the security clearance to do the work he'd done if anyone knew. And now there would always be a question.

He drained the glass, thought about throwing it against something, but he didn't want to have broken glass in the yard. "What did you and Kim plant?"

"Basil. We're going to have lots of pesto this summer."

In the dark, Gabriel reached out to him and took his hand.

CHAPTER 15

"I NEVER want you to regret loving me." Gabriel's hands were gentle, moving down his chest.

"How could I? That would be like regretting the way my heart beats." John felt a warm mouth tasting the skin of his neck, smelled the spicy, woodsy scent of Gabriel's hair, the sweat just under his hairline. "You've been the greatest joy in my life."

"And your life is getting really complicated since I moved my tools into your shed."

"Gabriel, don't talk. I've had enough talking for today, and we're not going to resolve anything. Let's just screw around."

That surprised a laugh out of him. "Yeah, okay. When all else fails, right?"

"Saved by the dick."

So many years, and the smell of his hair could still fill John's chest with heat, with need and longing that flowed down his spine like water. The ice that had sat in his belly since Martha told him what she'd done warmed, melted away under Gabriel's touch.

Gabriel had pushed the sheets to the end of the bed, settled himself on top of John, a hip over a hip, one long thigh nestled heavy and warm into John's groin, an arm thrown over his chest; his hand moving into the chest hair that was turning grayer by the day, and his head on John's shoulder, mouth an inch from the tender skin of his neck. John thought lying in his bed with Gabriel draped over him was as close to perfect as he was ever going to feel in this lifetime. And all Gabriel had to do was nudge him a little, move that long thigh against him.

"I've got you pinned down. I can do anything I want to you."

"Like what?"

"Hmmm, let me think." His hand was moving down John's belly, sliding, long fingers wrapping around him. "While I'm thinking, maybe I'll just take a taste."

"Good. That's a classic. Like Old Faithful." John put his hands behind his head and stared at the ceiling. He needed to think. He could tell Gabriel was smiling, felt his warm breath on his thigh, in and out, sweet, warm breath from the nose of the man he loved. John shook his head, checked the corners of the ceiling for cobwebs. *You are such a fool.* Then he thought he should tell Gabriel. "I am such a fool over you."

What was he going to do? It would be stupid to wait for the IG to approach him. By that time, decisions would have been made and pigheaded IG lawyers wouldn't back down, not once they'd taken a stand. So he would need to do some recon, just to get the lay of the land. And no way was Gabriel getting within a hundred miles of this one. If somebody needed to throw themselves off a cliff, John was going to make damn sure it was him. Gabriel had given enough.

"You're not really into this, are you?"

"Just thinking." He reached down, ran his fingers through Gabriel's hair. A year into retirement, and John suddenly felt like he'd been living in a giant protective army bubble, where nothing could hurt him, and he hadn't even realized it. Now he was out in the world, just another Joe Schmoe, and his importance to the big scheme of the world was less than that of the barista who had a coffee stand in the courtyard of the Pentagon. That was okay, there was a time for glory and a time to step down, but protecting himself from lawyers? Who could have imagined this? No, never in a million years had he considered this eventuality. He'd lived clean and worked hard and never crossed a line, never, not once, except for Gabriel. And that had never felt to him like a line he was crossing. It had felt like pure, sweet oxygen, when he'd been underwater for a couple of minutes too long. Lawyers were for the lazy scumbags who tried to slide the consequences of their weak characters under the radar. He realized he had his fingers in the hair of a lawyer who was breathing on his thigh, gave Gabriel a silent apology.

Gabriel scooted back to the head of the bed, pulled the sheet up over both of them. He squished his pillow around until it felt right, and then he settled in, stared at the side of John's head. John looked at him. "What?"

"Maybe we should talk about whatever it is you're thinking, General."

John shook his head. "Don't worry. I've got this one."

"I don't think so. You're not the Lone Ranger, and I sure as shit am not Tonto."

John lifted his head, stared at the man lying on the next pillow. "Excuse me?"

"I've always let you lead."

"Yes, well, I was the senior officer."

"Notice I used the past tense. You can still lead, John. You're smarter than me and more experienced and I trust you absolutely. I've had a whole lifetime of following your lead, and I don't know if I want to change now. But I'm the only attorney in this bed, and this is a legal matter that involves my wife and me. You've been caught up in it, but there is nothing here for you to handle. I'll take care of this."

"So I should just shut up and take my blowjob like a good boy, let you handle everything?"

"That would be fine with me."

"Are you really suggesting I should just stay at home, write some papers, watch the basil grow? Wait to be arrested, court-martialed, and stripped of my life's work?" John felt as close to speechless as he had ever been. "You...." He didn't know what to say, other than to put his hands over his face and scream.

"Nobody's going to arrest you. Don't you trust me to handle this? People pay me to do this for a living, remember? You think I'm going to let them get within ten miles of you?"

"Why do you say this has nothing to do with me? Did not your wife just name me as an adulterer? In a public, legal document? And, of course, Gabriel, she was right. We can't ignore the fact that she was correct. I did commit adultery. So did you. I mean, no one could argue the point that Martha has a legitimate grievance."

"'Women do most delight in revenge.' That was on my last fortune cookie at Ho Ho's. I'll argue the legitimacy of Martha's grievance at a later time. For now, let's get back to this one critical point. You don't trust me to protect you. Why not? Your back has been mine to watch since 1986, and now suddenly I'm not up to the task? Don't you know I would give my life to protect you? That I would give everything I have, everything I am, to protect you and keep you safe?"

John reached out, ran his hands down the angry, hurt lines of Gabriel's face. Gabriel closed his eyes, settled back into his pillow, and sighed. "Yes, I know what you would do for me. What you have always done for me." John started to speak, then stopped, lay back down, and stared at the ceiling again. "I've been a fool, and it's a miracle you've put up with me for all these years. The waiting, and the secrets. You gave up everything for this, for us, everything that mattered to you." He reached for Gabriel's hand, twined their fingers together. "Martha lost her family. You may lose that much, or more. But what have I given up? Where's my cost? Maybe there's a price for me to pay. I don't want you to have to give any more. It's my turn, don't you think?"

"No, I don't. That's ridiculous. You don't have to earn a place in my life. What, you think there's an entry fee? So much suffering is required to earn the right to love? It's not like that, John. It's just... totally fucking random. There is no reason to it, okay? Don't try and organize this into one of your outlines."

"Will you let me shake a few trees? See if I can get the old boys' network to gather some intel?"

Gabriel looked at him for a long moment. "Yeah, okay. That's probably the best way to proceed. Find out the mood, who's going to be making the decisions. Then we go in there and blow them out of the water."

"Agreed. I should see them before they decide to lay charges. Kim would be upset if I got arrested."

"Kim would be upset? I'll burn down the fucking brig. And no one is going to lay charges. I will have the ACLU boys standing before a bank of microphones, giving a press conference, before those dickheads finish printing out their charges. And you meant we, right? You said I would see them. You meant we would see them. Or I can put on my uniform and turn myself in first thing in the morning, and take care of this myself."

"I meant we. Always, Gabriel. We are a we. We aren't you and I anymore."

"Okay, good. As long as we're clear about that. Because I never want to have this conversation with you again. Ever."

"Would we have to play the gay card?"

Gabriel sighed. "John, we're gay. You know that, right?"

JOHN HEARD Kim in the kitchen making coffee, so he had time to pull the quilt up over them before he burst through the door. "So, Uncles! About time we had a counsel of war, don't you think?" He passed out coffee cups and settled himself, cross-legged, on the end of the bed. He nodded toward John. "I know you're King Arthur and I'm one of the knights, I think I want to be Lancelot, by the way, but even the knights have to have a briefing every once in a while. Just so they don't accidently stumble into the middle of an active op and screw things up." Gabriel blinked at him, took a sip of coffee. He looked sleepy, but John wasn't fooled. Pilots were up and in attack mode with zero warm-up.

"You heard from Billy?"

"He stayed with his dad at the Holiday Inn down by the airport. He sounded pretty small and sad. I'll tell you what I think. I think all you dads need to...." He stopped, the words drying up like a tiny stream in the heat of summer. "Okay! Never mind what I think. So what's happening?"

"About what?"

Kim frowned at him. "What is happening in your campaign to get Brian Walker fired?"

"Oh, that's done. Dean Fox had a letter of resignation for him yesterday. Or was it the day before?" He looked at Gabriel, but just got a gleam out of dark eyes and a grin. "And I believe the good dean also resigned yesterday."

"Who, George? Over this?"

"Over his recognized failure of leadership."

"So it's all done? You're finished?"

"Not quite."

Now Kim waited, arms folded across his chest, and John drank his coffee, waiting him out. Gabriel nudged him. "I would like to give Kim a briefing about what's happening with our family."

John looked at him in surprise. "Okay, if you think so."

"I think maybe Juan knew... he's been put in a bad position, regardless, and I want Kim to know what's going on." He held out his empty coffee cup. "I better get a refill before we start."

Kim collected coffee cups, went back into the kitchen. John leaned over, kissed Gabriel good morning. They were both sitting up against the headboard by the time Kim came back. He settled on the end of the bed again. "I think gay men should always do their problem solving naked and in bed."

John and Gabriel exchanged looks at this, and John sighed. "Must we have...?"

"Sorry, sorry! Just trying to lighten the mood. I get the feeling I'm not going to like whatever is coming."

Gabriel set down his coffee mug. "There are two situations that have dovetailed. Your uncle and I have been trying to figure out why Brian Walker has been protected by the university when they have known for some time he was abusive and having relationships with students. We uncovered information suggesting his father, Prentiss Walker, who is a member of the board of supervisors for the university system in New Mexico, has been protecting him through the university president, Simon Wainright. The report your uncle wrote regarding this matter went to a number of people who are on different sides of a political line up in Santa Fe. Walker, senior, has been threatened by the presence of this well-documented report, by his son's erratic and increasingly dangerous behavior, and by political rivals in the governor's office, who also have access to the report.

"Prentiss Walker has done two things. He has sent Brian into hiding, so he could not be arrested or fired, and I suspect is arranging some sort of rehab or medical admission, so he will be legally protected from action. The second thing he did...." He hesitated, and John could hear the strain in his voice. "He looked for a way to attack your uncle. Both distract him and attack his credibility. And the way he did that was he sent an attorney to Martha, and that attorney took a deposition regarding your uncle and my long-term affair, which was in violation of a number of statutes of the UCMJ, the Uniform Code of Military Justice. This deposition has been turned over to the inspector general, and if he follows usual procedures, their office will complete an investigation and then decide if they want to proceed to either court martial or administrative action against him. Against both of us."

"What sort of administrative action?"

"Reduction in rank, forfeiture of pension, fines."

"Are you fucking kidding me?" Kim had jumped off the bed, was pacing around the room, his hands bunched in his hair like he was going to snatch a handful by the root.

"Kiddo." His old nickname stopped Kim in his tracks, and he turned into his Uncle John's arms, tears spilling from his eyes. "You didn't think war was easy, did you?"

"I thought I was in grad school. When did that turn into a war?"

"I'm sorry, Kim." John stroked his dark hair. "You don't worry about it, honey. Let me and Gabriel handle everything. It will all be okay, I promise."

Kim pulled out of his arms. "I'm not a baby anymore! You have to let me help. I can't just go back to taking pictures...."

"That's exactly what you can do, and you will do. Kim, what I need is for everyone to do what they do best. Whatever you and Billy are planning for Ho Ho's? You make it outstanding. Make it mean something. It's a week Friday? Son, you understand we always need someone to lead the healing after the war has ended. That's your role. That's what I'm counting on you to do. You figure out a way to start us healing again. And I will take care of the rest of this mess."

Kim wiped the tears off his face with the back of his hand. "Okay. I can do that. You know, that sounds so corny, if anyone else but you had said it, I would think I was being played. But you really mean it, don't you?"

"Yes, I do."

After he left, Gabriel picked up his cup and took a thoughtful sip. "Nobody can play him like you can. You're King Arthur and Kim is Lancelot, so who the hell am I? You better not say Guinevere."

"You're the faithful consigliere. Always at my side."

"Ah. Okay, I'm good with that."

Kim stuck his head back in the door five minutes later. "Nobody asked me, but I bet I know where Brian is. He's got a boat down at Elephant Butte Lake. It's his favorite 'get out of town with the boys' toy."

Gabriel studied him. "No instructions not to approach? No lectures about dogs in this fight?"

Kim shook his head, and his face looked tougher than John had ever seen it. "He crossed a line when he attacked Billy. He crossed another one when his father attacked my family. Enough is fucking enough. You can punch me in the mouth, but he made a mistake when he went after my uncles, and my friend." Kim hesitated. "I just called Billy's dad, told him where to find Brian. I didn't want you to have to do that. Billy's coming over and we're going to work on the show while... while the warriors go to war."

151

CHAPTER 16

JOHN CALLED Charles Lathrop and told him he would be in Santa Fe and would like to come see him.

"I want to see you too, John. The kettle is set to boil over this mess. I talked to George Fox last night. He sounded like he'd been into the scotch, but I've never known him to drink."

"He had a blowup with Wainright. Maybe I'll see if he wants to come with us?"

"Sure, sure. Who else you bringing?"

"Gabriel Sanchez. My faithful consigliere."

"Oh, God. Now we've got the lawyers involved! Can you be here for lunch? I can probably take you boys out to lunch, so we can have a glass of wine and figure out a solution like civilized men."

John thought about Cody Dial, on his way to Elephant Butte to see Brian Walker, and about Billy Dial's young face. "Sounds good. Always best to stay civilized."

Gabriel was shaving in the bathroom. John leaned against the counter. "Bad news. We can't take the chopper up to Santa Fe. We need to take George Fox with us. Lathrop wants us to come for lunch. Can you be gone from work all day?"

Gabriel nodded. "No problem. I'll do some work tonight."

"You're putting a lot of time into this."

"Seems unlikely I'll ever be a wealthy barrister. I actually like the knuckleheads I end up defending. I wasn't expecting that. But they don't have any money. You don't mind, do you?"

John was surprised. "No, of course not. You've never been about money, and neither have I. We should have enough, don't you think?" He grinned at the sudden sharp pain in his gut. "Unless they take away my pension."

"Over my dead body," Gabriel promised. "Actually, I'm feeling quite free all of a sudden of the burden of giving Martha everything I have. I was planning to slave for the rest of my life to make it up to her, you know? Give her everything I had, other than myself. Now I think, screw it, she can go back to work like the rest of America and learn to live on a budget."

"She's a teacher, right?"

"Yep, and as far as I know, she's maintained her credentials, though she hasn't worked as a teacher since Juan was born. That little stunt just cost her half my retirement and half the equity in the house."

"Wear your Matrix-ninja killer suit today, okay?"

"You bet. I'm in the mood to kick some ass."

GEORGE FOX had been at the scotch the night before, but he was smooth and in control when they picked him up, just a tiny bit of bloodshot to the eye. They were both wearing navy-blue suits, George with a red tie and John with a blue. George put a drop of Visine in each eye, blotted them with a tissue. They smiled at each other. They were ready for battle.

Dr. Charles Lathrop was a large, charming man who loved to eat and drink, and he'd booked a table at The Plaza Cafe. "John! George! So pleased to see you both. And who is this?" Gabriel was introduced, and Lathrop took his arm in one of his big hands. "You have the look of a military man. Did you serve with the general?"

"I did. I retired from the army a few years ago, went back to law school."

"What do you think of the law? Does it compare to your military service?"

Gabriel shook his head slowly. "No. Not in any way. This is my soft little retirement career."

Lathrop looked at him in surprise, then glanced at John. "You military guys, you're so tough! That's why I love to see you coming into the academic world. Mix some good strong red blood in with all the blue."

John raised his eyebrows. Charlie Lathrop didn't come from the blue bloods. But Prentiss and Brian Walker did.

"George, I hope you've had a chance to rethink this resignation. I don't know what Simon would do without you. You're his right hand and his left hand, from what I've heard."

George shook his head. "Maybe I need to find a soft little retirement career too. Something easy. Maybe I could be one of those wrestlers. What do they call them? The ones who go into the cages and fight until someone's bloody and unconscious? That would be a nice break."

Lathrop sighed. It was clear this was not going to be an easy lunch. John smiled, pulled his napkin to his lap. "Charles, I read that article you wrote for *Foreign Affairs*. It was a subtle rethinking about the dynamics of Cuban-American relationships."

"Thank you, John! What have you been writing?"

"Xenophon again, off to *Monocle*."

"Always popular. We talked before about you writing a more extensive history of military leadership. Have you thought any more about that?"

"I've been tied up a bit, Charles, but that's always in the back of my mind. I'll need a year or more to do the research."

"Would you be interested in doing a few graduate seminars? Maybe one?"

John shook his head. "I'm not sure, Charles. Not... I'm not sure if I want to remain associated with this university system."

That dropped onto the table like a lead balloon, and they all stared at the tablecloth in silence. Their waiter, well trained in business lunches, moved in to pour wine and take orders and get them over the next few awkward minutes.

"Thank you for the report you sent, John." Charles put his reading glasses on, pulled out a memo pad and pen. He looked at George Fox. "And for your follow-up, George. Can you update me?"

George pulled his napkin into his lap, picked up his fork when the waiter slid a salad in front of him. "I told Simon I was going to terminate Brian Walker, as we discussed, and four hours later, Brian Walker disappeared."

"Have you been able to locate him and deliver the termination letter?"

"No."

"I suggest we let HR handle that from this point forward. You doing it was a courtesy, and his disappearance suggests we can withdraw the courtesy. Did Dr. Wainright say he had spoken to Professor Walker regarding the termination?"

George shook his head. "Claimed not to know anything about it, or his absence, though he did sign the medical leave papers. Maybe it happened when he was in a fugue state. Or one of those seizure disorders? What are they called, absence seizures? When you do things and later can't remember anything about it?"

Charles sighed, tapped the pen against the memo pad. "Could anyone else have gotten the information to Professor Walker? An admin?"

"Not sure." George ate a mouthful of salad. The look on his face suggested what he wanted to say was *I don't give a shit.*

Charles studied him for a moment, then put down the pen and picked up his fork. "Well, HR will manage things from this point, so I feel confident our students are...." He was looking at John. "How is your salad, John?"

John hadn't started to eat. He looked across the table, a cool gray gaze, his hands still in his lap. "Does Prentiss Walker have a reason to think he can manipulate personnel issues at the university from the board of supervisors?"

Lathrop rubbed his chin, then picked up his wine glass and took a sip. "There is certainly the appearance of inappropriate influence. I have concerns, and the governor shares those concerns. You can rest assured I'm gathering information." John didn't speak, and Charles gave him a crooked grin, drained his glass of wine. "He's going to be joining us for dessert, John. You can get a look at him then."

"Excellent." John picked up his fork. The salad was really quite good. "I'm sorry this problem got dumped into your lap, Charlie."

Charles shrugged. "It's the job, I guess. I don't know why people keep acting like fools and jackasses. I'm thinking about having one of those soft little retirement careers myself."

PRENTISS WALKER was a bluff, heavy man with a shock of carefully styled white hair and a face that was red enough John wondered about his alcohol intake and blood pressure. The waitstaff avoided him, leaving the hostess to greet him and escort him to their table. He looked powerful and spoiled. Charles Lathrop rose to shake hands, and he introduced the other men at the table. Walker studied Gabriel, then looked down at John. There was open derision on his red face. "So you brought the little boyfriend? He's your lawyer, huh? Isn't that sweet."

Gabriel stood up, looking lean and dark and dangerous, and stood between John and Walker. "Mr. Walker. Why don't you back way the hell off?"

Prentiss Walker grinned at Gabriel. "How's the little wifey?"

Gabriel was as still as stone. "You're about to make a mistake, sir, that you will bitterly regret."

"I doubt that." Walker turned away, studied Charlie Lathrop, then looked at John. "Now I am going to tell you all how things work in Santa Fe, and what we're going to do about this situation, so Charlie, you can get your little memo book out and take notes." He pulled up a chair, sat heavily. "General, you aren't a general any longer. We don't all jump when you yell. And you don't come into my back yard and start spraying like a tomcat and fucking with my son's career and reputation. So I'm going to tell you...."

John stopped listening, studied the plate of cheese and fruit. He was tired suddenly, tired of dealing with these weak men, these bullies and fools. Prentiss Walker was exactly what John thought he would be. Was there anyone who had the balls to be a better man than he had to be? He put his napkin down on the table and stood. George Fox stood, as well, taking his cue.

Charlie Lathrop looked startled. "Gentlemen, can we just sit down for a moment? Let's not...."

John shook his head. "I don't think that would be productive, Dr. Lathrop. You have the information you need for the governor to make a decision about this matter." John looked at Walker, studied him as the older man's face got redder and redder. Then he turned and walked out of the restaurant. Gabriel winked at Walker, which John thought might precipitate a stroke, and George Fox nodded to Lathrop, followed John and Gabriel out the door.

George didn't speak until they were in the car, and John could hear the grin in his voice. "Hey, that was kind of badass, wasn't it? I like how you military guys negotiate. So, what happens now?"

"Now we wait." John turned from the front seat. "That was a brilliant comment, by the way. You would be a wicked good cage fighter, George."

"Just a little fantasy of mine."

John looked at Gabriel. He was loose as a goose, his hand riding on the bottom of the steering wheel, looking through the CDs for some music for the ride home. His shoulders were moving to a familiar tune, and he was singing "Super Freak" under his breath.

John looked back at Fox. "The best negotiation is when you aren't negotiating."

CHAPTER 17

THE HOUSE was overrun with young artistic types running in and out of the garage, and John had to laugh at the noise they made, like a bunch of colorful tropical birds in too small a jungle. The boys and girls seemed to be dressed in rags or maybe curtains, not quite costumes, he thought, but he didn't want to ask and embarrass Kim by being so uncool.

John called Cody Dial, got him on his cell. "You still in town? I'm going to throw some steaks on the grill. You want to come over? We can drive down to Ho Ho's together for this shindig."

"I could eat a steak."

"I think Billy is already here. He was wearing a black cape a few minutes ago when he went by on his bike."

"A black cape? You know, his mama was an actress."

"I haven't talked to you for a couple of days. You happen to run into a man on a boat?"

"Such a pretty face the boy had. I offered to drop him off at the ER but he said no. I left him making up an ice pack, with blood and snot running down his chin."

"You like sirloin?"

"Yes, sir, I do."

CODY SHOWED up with a six-pack, passed out beers, and Gabriel showed him the cold frame, with the tiny basil seedlings popping up out of the black dirt.

He twisted the top off a beer. "I could use a couple of these cold frames up in Cheyenne. The winter gets ugly. You use wood screws to put it together?"

John had put their plates on a picnic table on the back porch so they could avoid the preparations for Ho Ho's. Gabriel set the table, and Cody sat on the porch, watching everyone, keeping an eye out for his boy. John brought the steaks to the table when they were done, and the three of them bent over their plates.

No one spoke until the last delicious tender bite was dispatched, then Cody pushed his plate away and sighed. "You know your way around a grill, General."

"I never asked you what you were doing now you've stopped bull riding."

"Ranching. Not much else to do in Wyoming other than roughnecking. I bought scrub ranchland with the money I earned riding."

"Cattle?"

Cody nodded. "Cattle and bison. I like those bison; they're tough sons of bitches. We've got close to a thousand acres. Sounds like more than it is. It's poor land, but we can squeeze a living out of it. My three oldest boys, they work it with me. It's funny. When I was riding, just before they opened the chute, with that monster between my legs, I used to think, no matter what else I do in my life, it won't be as hard as this. But I was wrong. Life just keeps getting harder. I try not to let my boys know. They'll find out soon enough, seems to me."

He looked out over the yard. Billy was wearing some sort of costume, a black skinsuit with sequins that looked like a white shirt, black tie and tux, with black Converse high tops. He had a top hat and a short black cape tied around his neck, and he swept the top hat off his

160

head, gave them a deep bow. "Billy, he never fit in with that bunch up there. He always had his eye set on something else. Someplace else. New Mexico. He talked about it all the time, the history, the artists. He was sure this was where he'd find a place to fit in."

Kim came out of the garage, looked at them sitting on the porch. He was shading his eyes with his hand, squinting up at them. His skinsuit was pink, with short legs that ended midthigh, and he was wearing pink Converse high-tops. He was wearing some sort of skirt over the skinsuit that looked torn and tattered, made out of pieces of gold lamé. His black hair was tied up in pigtails, and he gave them a little wave, pulled Billy away. John thought he could see pink nail polish. "Seems like he fits in pretty good with this bunch. Are they all artists?"

Gabriel nodded. "I got a look at the exhibit this morning. They've got several photographers, each with their own exhibit, a fiber artist, a mask maker and makeup artist—that's Billy—and a little three-man band. Three-person band, I guess. Drag queens." John and Cody exchanged a look. "These drag queens sing to support the victims of intimate partner violence. I think they call themselves the Kitty Cats."

"Well, I'll be looking forward to that," Cody said.

They stayed on the back porch for longer than they should have, telling war stories, stories about bull riding, stories about raising boys. Gabriel finally stood up. "If we miss the Kitty Cats opening number, we're going to be hearing about it for a very long time."

John found a parking space behind the McDonald's, and they pushed their way through the crowd of students and artists and homeless people to get into Ho Ho's. Out front, the huge banner for the art show was titled BEAUTIFUL FACES. The banner was a collage of children's faces, laughing, beautiful children's faces, babies, boys and girls, and along the bottom, the text gave statistics about intimate partner violence. John found the baby picture of Kim, his mouth grinning, drool on his chin. Cody pointed out a little picture of Billy in a red cowboy hat.

Inside, the artist-hosts had been painted up by Billy's hand to look like cats. Gabriel nudged him. "It's from that musical *Cats*.

Remember? Billy is the Magical Mr. Mistoffelees, and Kim is Grizabella. Look at the old ladies."

The elderly Vietnamese ladies were serving up food in twin cat costumes. John shrugged, looked a question at Gabriel. "Mungojerrie and Rumpleteaser?" Gabriel was studying the crowd, and John thought he was watching for Juan. They spotted him finally in a tan trench coat and rumpled hat, with cat whiskers glued on his nose. Gabriel grinned. "He's Macavity, the Mystery Cat." He pushed through the crowd until he was in front of Juan. The Mystery Cat let him have a hug; then he wiggled away and was off again, delivering his trays of food.

The Kitty Cats were a trio of pretty ladies with extravagantly long painted nails, two blondes and a redhead, wearing black stockings and heels. They sang a variety of doo-wop songs that were easy to dance to and showed off their wide range of voices to good effect.

They walked along the walls, looking at the exhibits. John saw Kim's photography immediately. The group was titled *The Blueberry Chronicles!* He had done a series of self-portraits, then marked them up with magic marker comments. One picture showed his swollen, cut lip, pushed out with his tongue, and the magic marker said, *Ow! That hurts!*

The blueberry picture was there, and Kim posed as Rodin's *The Thinker*, and the thought bubble over his head said, *What the Fuck Just Happened?*

The one John liked the most was Kim with a mad face, mad, but with sad eyes, and he'd made a list at the bottom of the photograph. *Options*, it said. *1. Buy a Weapon. 2. Have a Good Cry. 3. Talk to the Cops? 4. Get a Facial. 5. All of the Above.*

One of the other photographers had printed photos on fabric, then washed them until they were faded and torn. The fabric artist had made something that looked like little baskets with pieces of metal sticking out from the sides. These were titled *Wreck on the Highway*. All of the work had edges that were torn, frayed, worn-out. Billy had made a series of masks that were hanging on the wall, and Gabriel studied these a long time. They looked Japanese, and Gabriel told John and Cody they were faithful depictions of ancient samurai helmets made out of paper, and they showed cuts and tears, like they had been used in battle. Billy came up to them, his face painted black and white. He was wearing the mask John thought made him look like the Phantom of the Opera. "I'm real proud of you, son." Cody gathered him up close, and Billy snuggled happily in his father's arms.

"I just felt like I wanted everybody to have a helmet when they needed one."

A reporter came up to them, a young girl with intense dark eyes. She gave Gabriel a hungry look and dragged him away into the corner for a chat. John saw her showing him a copy of what looked like a cell phone picture from Effex, with the banner of Brian Walker's face. She was talking, gesturing, and Gabriel had his hands in his pockets, staring out into space. He turned around, looked back at John, winked, then leaned over and spoke in her ear for a good two minutes. She was smart enough to be quiet and listen, and John hoped she had a recorder on her person somewhere, so she didn't miss anything.

They ducked out when the Kitty Cats were starting their second set. They left Billy and Kim dancing in the middle of the floor, Kim's torn gold lamé skirt flying out when he spun on his pink sneakers.

JOHN LOOKED into the garage early. Kim was splayed across his bed, facedown, still wearing his gold skirt and pink skinsuit. Billy was there too, curled up on a couple of pillows, and there were three other artists, cats, or drag queens, John wasn't sure, lying on the floor, asleep. They looked like a piece of performance art, gay angels after the fall. John closed the door again and put on a big pot of coffee.

He heard the shower come on a few minutes later, and Billy peeked through the door, wearing one of Kim's tee shirts and a pair of sweats that fell over the top of his feet. John got him a tea bag and the unfiltered raw honey.

"I really loved the show, Billy. You guys did a great job."

"Gabriel said he wanted to buy the masks! Isn't that cool? My first professional art sale."

"Very cool." He waited, and Billy sipped his tea.

"I don't know if I should go home with my dad. I mean, this is just one setback, right? I'll have others. I need to figure out how to handle the things that come my way." John waited. "On the other hand, I'm only eighteen. I have to admit I've been more homesick than I expected to be. I know my mom is worried."

"What would you do if you went home?"

"There's a decent art school at the U. Heavy into cowboy art, though. Realistic art, not a great deal of abstraction. I'm totally into the abstract. I'm not sure how well I'd fit in there." He looked back at the garage. "I fit in really well here. Really, really well. Like the cat's pajamas."

"You going to talk to your dad?"

"Yeah."

"Tell him I said you could stay here with us."

Billy's face bloomed into a smile. "Really? That would be so cool! Even though I know I'm going to be like an annoying little brother to Kim. He can be really protective, you know? One of those Kitty Cats asked me out, the one with the red hair, and Kim was, like, right there, and he made some joke about my being too young and led me away by the wrist! Can you believe that?"

"Those Kitty Cats looked a bit too old to me too."

Billy shrugged. "Older guys have always asked me out. This was the first drag queen, though. I actually think she was trying to recruit me into the band. How cool would that be?"

"You talk to your dad, and then let me know." John was running through available bedrooms in his mind.

Kim staggered into the kitchen, holding his head between both hands. He appeared to have lipstick smeared across his face, and he was greenish under the pancake. John studied him without speaking, his arms crossed over his chest. "Don't go anywhere," Kim said, and he sprinted to the bathroom. John heard some retching, then the water running.

Billy was shaking his head. "There is too much alcohol in the gay college scene," he said, trying on the mask of a wise old sage. John gave him a look, and he giggled and went back to the garage. "I'm getting dressed and going off to see my dad," he said. "Later, gator."

Gabriel came out of the bedroom dressed for work, wearing a new lavender shirt and a purple-and-gray silk tie. John felt a little twist of lust when Gabriel grinned at him, tucked his shirt in his waistband.

"You want some coffee?"

Gabriel slid his hands around John's waist. He leaned down, nibbled his way along his jawline. "I want something."

"I just offered young Billy a berth with us. We may have to think about building an addition on to the house."

"I bought his masks for our bedroom."

"Yeah, he told me. He's really psyched."

"I'm probably going to be late tonight. I've got some work to catch up with. Anyone calls you from the IG's office, call me right away, okay?"

"No worries there. I might drop dead from a heart attack."

Gabriel look at him a long moment. "Have you talked to Kim this morning?"

"He staggered in here, then went off to puke."

"I think he's got an idea we might consider. I'm going to leave it to you, but my vote is yes." Gabriel kissed him before he could speak, grabbed his briefcase off the table, and was out the door.

Kim was back a few minutes later, holding a file folder. He sat down at the kitchen table, rested his head on the tabletop. "That was an absolute frigging blowout! What did you think?"

"I thought it was an absolute frigging blowout. I'm real proud of you, kiddo."

"One of the galleries downtown said they want to host the show. That is un-fucking-believable! My first curated show."

"Very cool."

"So I've been thinking about your issue with Mrs. Horse-Lord. And all that it entails regarding your future and your past."

"Not your problem, Kim."

"Just listen. You remember the picture I took of you and the Horse-Lord?" John nodded. Kim pulled a photograph out of the folder and showed it to him. They were laughing, their arms around each other, Gabriel looking dark and fierce and handsome in his flight suit. John's gray eyes were lit with laughter. "Now look at this."

Kim pulled another photo out of the folder. It was a copy of the same picture, but it had been mocked up to resemble a magazine cover. At the very top was the word OUT, and along the bottom, the words: *The General and the Horse-Lord. The Army Comes Out of the Closet.* "I don't know if you've ever read *Out*, but it's the premiere magazine for the gay community. I want you to consider doing an interview with them about what it was like to be on active duty when it was illegal to be gay. How it affected your life, your choices. And what's happening now, how those times are still being used against you."

John stared down at the photograph, imagined seeing that picture on the cover of a magazine sold all over the country. Maybe all over the world. Coming out to the world. Gabriel, saying his vote was yes.

"What it would mean is you get to tell your side of things. No one can threaten you with something if you take ownership of it. And this will keep the inspector general from even thinking about proceeding against you. You've already been a hero, and now you'll be a gay hero, risking it all for love. They can't be seen to attack a hero."

"Kim, what makes you think this magazine would be interested in an interview like this?"

"I already contacted them. I sent them a copy of the photo and gave the reporter a little brief. Who I was, who you are, who Gabriel is. I offered to write the story myself. They said they would send their own people, but they would use my photo. That's a major coup for a young photographer such as myself. But now I'm thinking how much fun it is to stage art shows. Maybe I should be a gallery slave. But what would Ho Ho's do without me?"

"Kim? You already contacted them? Without speaking to me first?"

"Uncle John, sometimes you're a little slow on the uptake. You need a gentle push in the right direction."

"You think so?"

"The Horse-Lord wants full disclosure. He wants to live in the light, openly and honestly, with you. You can see that, can't you? But he would never push you. You could give him this gift. And if you do this, you remove a weapon from your enemy. Good strategy, right?"

"It's a tactic we could consider," he said. "I'll think about it. Now, on to another topic. Billy's off talking to his dad about staying here for school. What's your take?"

"He's still a little frail, but he's a good artist, Uncle John. I really hope he gets his chance. He's just so open, you know?" Kim was frowning. "He's a little too open to people. He'll go off with anybody. He says artists have to have a broad range of experiences. I mean, shit, *Juan* is more careful about strangers!"

"I told him he could stay here with us. We could build another studio in the garage if you guys could share the bathroom."

Kim shook his head. "There's plenty of room. We could share the garage as is without any problem. If you built another studio, we'd spend all our time tapping out messages on the walls between our spaces. Billy likes to talk, have you noticed that?"

"No, really?"

"Where I've got all my art supplies, we could clear that out and put in a bed and desk. We actually have access to studio space at the school. And that way I can keep an eye on him. But what about Juan?"

"I was thinking about moving the office into the dining room. We hardly ever use that dining room, and we can eat in the kitchen on Thanksgiving. It's big enough for me and Gabriel to have workspace. That would free up two bedrooms, so each of the kids could have their own. He was Macavity, the Mystery Cat?"

"I can't believe you knew that!"

"Gabriel told me."

"You left before my soliloquy. Grizabella sings a really famous song. Want to hear?"

"I've heard you sing before, kiddo. But yes, I want to hear your song. Always and forever."

JOHN WAS studying the dining room, trying to figure out where he could fit the desks, when George Fox called. "Hey, John. You left last night before the Kitty Cats did their Elvis medley!"

"Oh. Sorry I missed that, George. How are things with you?"

"Good. I just got a call from Charlie Lathrop's assistant, asking me to take a drive up to Santa Fe and see him. How about them apples?"

"If he's got a brain in his head, he'll be begging you to take over some potential disaster of a school. What do you think?"

"I did have a friend at New Mexico Tech mention the vice president's position down there is vacant. No one's wanted it because the president has such a reputation. Stainless-steel balls and all that."

"I thought the president at New Mexico Tech was a woman?"

"Yeah, she is. That's the point."

"Ah. That might be a fun job, George. Maybe he's giving you some experience before the next president's job opens."

"Maybe. I'll see what he says. But I'm going to remember your negotiating advice, John. I could always retire, spend the next few years travelling. My wife has mentioned how much she would like to do that very thing. Are you going to work on that book you were talking about with Charlie?"

"Maybe. Seems I've got a lot of family things going on right now. I need for life to settle down a bit. Then I can get to work."

"I'll give you a call when I hear anything. Oh, did you see that girl reporter last night? She was hot on the trail of a story, looking for a cover-up and political malfeasance. She's a nice girl." George sighed. "Her mother was one of my favorite students when I was still in the classroom. Seems like just yesterday."

"I did see her. She was wearing a trench coat and carrying a little memo pad?"

"Yeah. I hear she's got the front page byline of the student newspaper whenever she wants it."

"Interesting. Well, I'll be looking forward to seeing what she comes up with. Good luck, George."

Cody Dial knocked on the door in time to help him move the dining room table out to the shed.

"I had a feeling things were going this way when I saw how happy he was last night."

"He told you I said he could stay here?"

Cody nodded. "I thought I would help you move some furniture." They looked into the garage, and both shook their heads over the clothes scattered across the floor and dripping off the bed.

"Kim said we could move those art supplies out, and put a bed and desk in that corner for Billy."

Cody nodded. "That would work. You tell Billy a fair price for rent, and make sure you collect. I don't want him to get the idea he can sleep somewhere for free. He's got scholarship money." He looked around again. "I'll run out, get a bed and a desk. Maybe a little dresser for his clothes. I'll be back in a couple of hours."

"I'll go with you if I can. I need to pick up a second desk for Gabriel. I'm going to set us up an office in the dining room."

"Gabriel has a couple of kids?"

"Yeah. A girl, eight, and a son who's fourteen. You met him last night."

"Boy's got a big chip on his shoulder."

"Yes, he does."

They climbed into Cody's pickup truck, and John saw a black sedan with dark windows turn the corner and drive slowly down his street as they were pulling out of the driveway. His heart seized up a bit, his stomach filling with ice. It looked like a government vehicle. Was the inspector general coming to read charges against him? He could be arrested, pending reinstatement on active duty and court-martial. John couldn't believe this was actually a possibility. What was worse, he felt shaky and weak, like his foundations were crumbling. If he wasn't General Mitchel, he didn't know who he was. He thought about what Martha had said to him about burning his life to the ground. It felt like she might get her wish.

CHAPTER 18

CODY DIAL was as helpless as John was in a furniture store, or maybe more, if that was possible. They stared around at desks made out of glass and metal and old-fashioned cherry wood and antique look-alikes. John threw up his hands. "We've got Kim and Billy and *we're* trying to decorate? Why don't I give them a thousand bucks and let them go shopping?" He looked at a few more price tags. "Maybe fifteen hundred bucks."

"I can throw Billy some spending money." Cody spotted the kid's quilts and blankets, bought Billy a quilt covered with little horses and boots and cowboy hats. It looked like a bedspread for a five-year-old who had just decided he wanted to be a cowboy when he grew up. It came with a little rug shaped like a cowboy boot. "Trust me, he'll love it. You haven't seen his collection of boots. Billy looks at cowboys and sees style. I look at cowboys and see hard work that needs to be done."

"I'll keep an eye on things if you need to get home."

Cody sighed. "I'm getting a bit itchy being in the city. Seems the city is full of people who talk before they think just to fill up the quiet." He looked over at John. "Present company excepted. You and Gabriel come on up and ride, you get a notion to spend some time on a horse."

"Thank you, maybe we will. Gabriel would fly his little helicopter up to Cheyenne at the drop of a hat."

"What did he fly in the army?"

"Apache attack helo. AH-64."

"That the one with the big rocket launcher?"

"You bet."

"He looks like a man who would not hesitate to pull the trigger, he's got an enemy lined up in his sights. I'm the same way myself."

Cody dropped the bedspread and rug in the garage, went off to find Billy and say good-bye. Kim was at Ho Ho's doing the prep. They'd stayed late the night before, cleaning up from the show. The front windows looked cleaner than John had ever seen them. Kim brought him a pot of tea. "You want some soup, Uncle John?"

He shook his head. "Could I talk you into buying furniture? Doing some decorating?"

Kim's dark eyes went big. "The first thing we throw out is that ratty old couch and get something in leather, maybe cream-colored leather!"

"What's wrong with the couch? The couch is fine. I was thinking about a couple of desks for me and Gabriel in the dining room, and furniture for Billy in the garage. We might have to make up rooms for the kids, like lavender walls for Martie? Or pink?"

"So you were thinking about a couple of beautiful and functional rooms, and leave the rest of the house looking like a barracks?" Kim shrugged. "Okay, okay, whatever you want. What's the budget?"

"A thousand bucks?"

Kim burst out laughing. "Are we shopping at Goodwill?" He was giggling when he went back behind the serving counter, clutching John's Visa card. John made a note to call Navy Federal Credit Union and tell them he was going to be making some big purchases.

John went out running, made a longer loop than usual, thinking about Gabriel. Gabriel voted yes, but he was leaving it up to him. Of course he was. He always had. But John understood clearly what he wanted. He thought maybe it was the first time Gabriel had ever asked him for anything, other than a shed to store his tools. And it felt like he was asking for the world.

What did John value most? Loyalty. Privacy. The privacy felt critical to him, like it was essential for his life to stay on an even keel, to keeping his balance in an off-balance world. But even more than that, he'd valued the quiet, private times with Gabriel though the years. They'd made a secret garden, filled with peace, and time out of world, and love. It was those times that he could feel in his mind, their warmth and brightness, like they held some light the rest of his life did not.

So there was no question what he was going to do. Gabriel had never asked him for anything, and it was inconceivable John would say no. But how? Did he need to be concerned about tactical advantage? One of the best lessons for the warrior-philosopher was to gather like-minded warriors to the cause so one was not fighting alone. George Fox was a warrior, though he was only now learning the difference between politics and leadership. Charlie Lathrop was still a question. Cody Dial? A warrior, no question, but he'd played his part and retired from the battle. The young student reporter? They would have to see what she did with the information she'd gathered. Kim and Billy? Beautiful, gentle souls. He thought of their art show, felt a warm bloom of affection for the kindness of their worldview.

Now, on to his personal war, his and Gabriel's. Gabriel could be at risk as well from an IG investigation, but they would never go after him without going after the general first. John didn't have a feeling for the mood at the IG. Sometimes they wanted to be seen to be very supportive and caring about the concerns of military spouses. Other times they took a hard line and protected their service members. No one would confuse this gambit as anything but the bitterness of a soon to be ex-spouse. Gabriel was going to research the current members of the IG's office to see if there was anyone they knew. The thought of pulling some strings to keep himself from a personal scandal caused his stomach to twist into an ugly little knot. Who knew Martha had such a vindictive heart? By the time she calmed down, and decided to regret playing for revenge, it would be too late. Gabriel wouldn't forgive this. Maybe she wouldn't, either.

Out. What would it be like to talk to a reporter, to talk about being gay and in the military? It seemed to be a betrayal, but was it really? Would the old boys who had always supported him still have supported him if they had known? Was he a different person, a stranger, the gay general, or was he the person he'd always seemed to be? And Gabriel voted yes. Maybe what he needed to do was go talk to one of his mentors, to one of the old men who had depended on him to solve their thorniest problems. Now he had a problem of his own, and he wondered what their advice would be. *Out* or in?

HE SENT Gabriel an email with one word: YES. He called Kim, who was with Billy in a furniture store downtown. "Yo, Uncle J, what's the credit limit on this thing? Twelve thousand?"

He was silent, waited him out.

"Okay, okay, just kidding. You're going to be *amazed*!"

"I always am. Call your friend at *Out* and tell him I said yes."

"Holy shit!" Kim was breathing into the phone. "I can't believe it! I never thought you'd do it. Man, I owe Billy ten bucks!"

"I may be late. Keep your Uncle Horse-Lord company, and I better not come home to find a new couch in the living room."

"So where are you going?"

John hung up the phone. He gave Charlie Lathrop a call. "You and I need to go see Governor Martinez today." He listened to Charlie breathe.

"John, it's more complicated than that. I can't just demand she...."

"I speak to her today, or I speak to a reporter. Today."

"Okay, John. I hear you. I've just been.... What's your schedule look like?"

"I'll be in Santa Fe at three," John said.

"Did you hear? Prentiss Walker is down in Albuquerque. Seems he's had to put Brian into the hospital for rehab. Word is alcohol, but it always is down there in cowboy country. My guess is he's got some preacher in there praying over Brian so he'll stop looking at boys."

"I hadn't heard." He thought a moment. He hated to leave town with Prentiss Walker near his boys. Well, Gabriel could look out for them if a problem cropped up. "Okay, I'll see you at your office at three."

Governor Martinez was rushed, and had obviously carved some unplanned time out of her busy day to see them. She slowed down, though, when she started going through the updated report John slid across her desk. She read carefully, then looked up at Charlie. "Does the media have this?"

"Not that I know."

"Maybe," John said. They both looked at him. "A young student reporter attended the art show on Friday. She had some independent information about the two most recent assaults on students." He paused. "I understand the student newspaper comes out tomorrow."

"Charlie, how could this go on for so long?" The governor's jaw was getting tight.

Charlie adjusted his suit coat. It looked to John like it was getting small across the shoulders. "We have no proof that would stand up in court, but the preponderance of evidence suggests that Simon Wainright was shielding Brian Walker from complaints made by these boys he was dating."

"These boys he was hitting, you mean." John looked steadily at Charlie. "Students he was sleeping with and hitting."

"That's not dating where I come from. And gay or not, adults or not, the relationship between a teacher and a student is never appropriate." The governor's face was turning pink with fury. "What possible reason would Simon Wainright have for protecting this man? At the request of his father? Do we have any evidence that suggests Prentiss Walker was influencing events, or are we just guessing?"

"No," Charlie said. "We don't really know."

"Has anyone actually asked Simon why he made these personnel choices?" John looked at the governor. She was petite, shorter than she looked on TV, and tougher, her hair styled in a careful bob. He could see her behind the controls of an Apache attack helicopter, her thumb on the button.

The governor looked pointedly at Charlie.

"Actually, we've been playing phone tag. I haven't been able to speak to him."

"Phone tag. I see." She looked at John, breathing deeply, like she was composing herself. "General Mitchel, thank you for the information. Charlie, I want a board of supervisor's meeting called tonight. I'll attend, and we will discuss emergency suspension for the president of the university. The attorney general's office can complete the investigation and decide if they want to bring action." She turned to her aide. "Make sure the attorney general attends, and give him a copy of this report." She turned back to John. "I'm sure, General, that their recommendations will be in line with yours." She stood up, held out her hand, and John shook it, followed Charlie Lathrop from the office.

"She's a tough little cookie," John said. "She ever in the service?"

Charlie shook his head, clapped him on the shoulder. "She just had a public fight with her hairdresser over gay marriage, so now she's got to be seen to support the gay community. They're everywhere in Santa Fe."

"Really? Maybe they're just everywhere, Charlie."

"Some days, no matter what I say, somebody is going to be pissed off." Charlie stopped on the steps, and the wind blew open his suit coat. It smelled dry and green, like sage and roasting chili peppers. "I really hate politics in this century. Go write something good and leave me in peace, John, okay?"

"Maybe I will."

JOHN DROVE out toward Los Alamos to see an old friend. Admiral Mike Adams had recruited John for his last assignment to the Joint Chiefs as senior aide for Strategy and Tactics. They had known each other for more than thirty years, since they had served together at the Joint Command. Mike had invited him up to see his place when he called, said he was bored to death with his bonsai.

John had to grin at the solar greenhouse and the rows of bonsai lined up like little soldiers. Or little sailors, lining the deck of an aircraft carrier. "It's about eight thousand square feet," Mike said, showing him the automatic watering system and the solar fans. "Once I got started, things just got out of hand. My wife says I have to start selling some of the plants. She wants me to sell them at the farmer's market."

They looked at each other, shaking their heads. Selling bonsai at the farmer's market. Teaching lazy freshmen the basics of civics. Who was providing leadership to the world, since they had stepped off the merry-go-round? Mike looked relaxed, though, his gray hair overgrown and wild around his head, wearing an old Navy sweatshirt and a frayed pair of khakis.

John pulled out the photo of Gabriel and him, the one Kim had mocked up like the magazine cover. Mike studied it. "That's your pilot, right? The one they called the Horse-Lord? What's his name again?"

"Sanchez. Gabriel Sanchez. He went to law school when he retired, took the bar. He's in practice down in Albuquerque."

"Sanchez, that's right. He was always like a junkyard dog, watching your back. Nobody got near the general when the Horse-Lord was around."

John wasn't sure his old friend was picking up the message. "Mike, this is a magazine cover. *Out* is a gay magazine. They want to interview us."

"I know, John. My youngest son is gay. He leaves *Out* lying all over the house for me to read. They have ads for the strangest shoes I've ever seen. I mean, orange oxfords? What sort of pants...."

"Mike, did you know I was gay?" His throat nearly closed, and he realized he'd said it out loud for the first time.

Mike was studying one of his little bonsai trees, reached into the pocket of his old khakis, and took out a pair of scissors. He took a tiny snip from a branch. "Always lots of confirmed bachelors in the military. Some people have to give up having a family to serve."

"Will there be any question about the work when this comes out? I'm concerned. I don't want there to be any question...."

"John, no. Impossible. No one would ever question your ethics. You were the gold standard of ethical behavior. The rest of us just tried to measure up to the bar you set."

"I think the IG is going to lay charges against me." His voice cracked, and he gestured to the picture. "Gabriel's wife. He asked her for a divorce. She went out and bought a big gun."

Mike grinned at him. "Don't piss off the wives. Rule number one. But in your case, John, I think you've given enough. You deserve to have your Horse-Lord after all these years. Don't you think? I've got an old friend in the IG's office. I'll see what's up." He lifted the tiny pine tree in its clay pot. "Don't worry so much, John. I've got your back. Take this one home. I can tell the wife I sold it. I think she's got them numbered."

He pulled out a small memo book from his pocket, flipped to a clean page. "I'm writing down the name of an attorney. You and the Horse-Lord, you call this guy, make an appointment. Let him contact the IG and get a copy of the dep and find out what's happening. This guy's an ass, but you don't have to like him. Then you go in to see them. Make sure the IG knows you're going to talk to those reporters at *Out*. And I'll give my old fishing buddy a call."

JOHN DROVE home in the quiet dark, the road twisting through the arroyos and mesas between Los Alamos and Albuquerque, the little bonsai buckled into the passenger seat. He was making an outline in his mind, a problem-solving tool he'd used since his early days as a civil engineer, designing roads and bridges over shifting sand. He had a nagging feeling something was missing, something left undone. Maybe it was just terror at what Kim and Billy had done with his credit card.

He made a mental list, checked everything off as completed or resolved, until he got to Brian Walker. In rehab, Charlie Lathrop had told him. Where? Had the information been independently confirmed? It had been nearly a week since Cody had given him a beat-down. Prentiss Walker. He'd have been notified about the emergency board of supervisor's meeting, and the topic of the meeting, the planned presence of the governor and the attorney general. He would have some idea what it meant. Where was Prentiss Walker?

Charlie would never feed him false information deliberately, though John had to admit the man had been less helpful than he had anticipated. He seemed a bit overwhelmed by the new position. Well, scholarship and leadership were not always two sides of the same coin. And if he was being honest, John thought he had detected a change in the man's attitude toward him. Maybe Charlie Lathrop didn't like him anymore because he'd heard through the grapevine that John was gay. He felt a little pang in his stomach. Had he been living his quiet life this way because he wanted people to like him, and he thought maybe they wouldn't if they found out he was gay? It was an interesting thought he would have to explore in more detail at a later date, when the current crisis was put to bed.

Could someone have manipulated Charlie, given him the information about Brian Walker going into rehab, hoping he would pass it along to John? What would be the point? Why would Brian want John to think he was safely out of the way? Because then he would not be standing watch over Billy and Kim, protecting them.

He pulled out his phone, dialed Gabriel. "Where are you? There's trouble."

"At home. Moving furniture."

Thank God. "Are Kim and Billy with you?"

"No, they're up at Ho Ho's."

"Gabriel, I don't know where Brian is. I was told he went into rehab but the information hasn't been confirmed. The governor is calling a meeting of the board of supervisors tonight to suspend Wainright."

"I'm on my way."

"Be careful."

"No worries. I'll call when I've got them safe."

JOHN WAS ten miles from Albuquerque when Gabriel called back. "Ho Ho's is busy, no hostiles in evidence."

"Can you get Kim to go home with you?"

"Negative. He's working the wok. Billy's with me. Juan is here too, bussing tables."

"I'm almost there."

"Roger that."

JOHN BROKE several traffic laws getting to Ho Ho's, dread filling his stomach. All his boys were in the danger zone. He parked at the McDonald's again, sprinted across the street. He slowed when he got near the door, scanned the parking lot for cars that looked out of place among Ho Ho's usual crowd. There were a couple of homeless guys sitting on the curb, and several students walking down Yale. The deli on the right side of Ho Ho's looked like business as usual, and Ho Ho's had three people in line at the glass serving counter. One of the Vietnamese ladies was dishing up tongfuls of noodles into a line of Styrofoam containers.

Kim was visible behind the counter, back to the customers, bent over a steaming wok, as Gabriel had said. Billy was sitting at a table in the back with Gabriel and Juan, looking around, anxiety on his face. The bruises were faded, but still visible. He had his arms wrapped around himself. Juan had his head down on his folded arms, playing his Nintendo. Gabriel was sitting with his back to the corner of the room, his chair tilted back, scanning the room. He was cool as ice.

It looked like the usual crowd when John opened the door and pushed into the room. There was a group of students in the back corner by the bathroom, the girls talking and texting, the guys working on mouthfuls of noodles. The hand-printed sign at the counter said, "Special, Noodles. $2.49." Kim turned around, dumped a pile of noodles into the steam tray on the serving line. He looked up and saw John, smiled at him, and then he looked past him, the smile falling away, his face still and white. John felt the arm lock around his neck, and Brian Walker breathed scotch fumes into his ear. "Well, well, it's Uncle General, come running to the rescue."

John stepped back to throw Brian off balance, but Brian anticipated the move. "Don't worry. It's not you I've come for." He let

179

go of John, pushed him forward into a table, and spun around. Gabriel was right behind him, moving forward, and Brian pointed his gun at Gabriel's forehead. The gun was tiny, fancy silver filigree on a twenty-two that fit into his hand.

Gabriel put up his hands and grinned at the gun. "What, is that a toy? Do you even know how to put bullets in that little bitty thing?"

Billy was sickly white, clinging to the tabletop, but Juan was up and moving across the restaurant toward his dad, his fists clenching, his jaw shoved out like a little bulldog. Billy jumped up and ran after him. "Juan, no! Don't go near him. He's dangerous." Billy was crying now. "He's a fucking asshole, that's what he is. An asshole, and a mediocre artist. He's got about as much talent as he can hold in his stupid little fists." John held up a hand to stop them both from coming any closer.

Brian Walker ignored Billy. He was weaving on his feet, the gun moving between Gabriel and John. "It took me a few days to figure out what would be the biggest kick in the balls for you, General. But I figured it out, didn't I? I've been waiting for you to get here so you could watch." His face was purple and swollen, nose broken, one eye closed and eyebrow cut, and it looked like a tooth had cut through his upper lip. How had Cody managed to replicate so perfectly the beating the man had given Billy? "You couldn't bear to lose your man, could you?"

He must have been sitting in his car, drinking, waiting for John to show. John wondered if he was going to fall down drunk before one of them had the chance to punch him out.

John wanted to keep Brian looking at him, give Gabriel a chance to get the gun safely away from him. "You go after the boys filled with light, don't you, Brian? The happy ones, the boys who accept themselves. The boys who have fathers who love them. Fathers who adore them, in all their beautiful colors. It must just shine out of them, all that love, and all you can think to do is try to turn their light to darkness. I don't know why it took me so long to see it."

Brian was snarling, the part of his face that wasn't already swollen turning bright red. The hand holding the gun was shaking.

"What did your father do to you? And why couldn't you be man enough to rise above it? You could have been anything. Done anything with your life. So much potential wasted. And it's too late now."

Brian's teeth were chattering with rage. "You don't know me. You don't know anything...."

"I know you just used a handgun in the commission of a felony." John's voice was quiet. "In front of witnesses."

Brian's face blanched, and Gabriel reached over, twisted his wrist until he dropped the little gun. Gabriel twisted harder, and Brian dropped to his knees.

"What the fuck is wrong with you?" Gabriel said. "Did you just wave a gun around in front of my son? Are you kidding me?" Juan ran to his father, wrapped his arms around Gabriel's waist, and buried his face in his shirtfront.

Kim threw his wok over the glass serving counter, sprayed Brian with noodles and sesame oil and pieces of diced carrots. The wok bounced off his head with a hollow thud. Then the two Vietnamese ladies were out from behind the serving line like a flash, beating on Brian with their tiny fists, screaming at him, and Gabriel handed John the gun. John stuck it in his pocket, looked back at the girls huddled in the corner. One of them slid out of the booth and held her phone up like Lady Liberty. "I've called 911!"

Brian tried to stand, but Gabriel was looming over him. "Don't even think about it." He had his arm around Juan, and he beckoned Billy over, wrapped both of them up close to his chest. "Nothing to be scared about, boys."

Billy narrowed his eyes at the man on the floor, pulled his foot back, but then he hesitated, didn't kick him. He put his head back down on Gabriel's chest, closed his eyes. Juan patted him awkwardly on the shoulder.

Brian sneered up at him. "What a sweet little ass. What's your name again?"

Billy turned his head, looked down at the man on the floor, then reared back and kicked him in the balls. Or tried to. He mostly hit Brian's upper thigh, and it was a symbolic gesture at best. John gave him a thumbs-up.

John looked at Kim. "What was the point of throwing the wok?"

Kim shrugged. "It made me feel better. Like I was contributing."

"Now we've got oil on the floor. Okay, how much?"

Kim blinked a few times. "Nearly seven thousand. Okay, I'll tell you the truth. Just over seven thousand. But that includes all the paint and equipment we need to repaint the living room and kitchen." He looked at John closely, like he was getting ready to catch him if he fell. "Billy's going to make the new curtains, so that will save some money. And if you don't like the new couch, you can take it back. But you won't. You're going to love it, I swear."

"Seven *thousand*?" For the first time all night, John found himself ready to hyperventilate.

CHAPTER 19

JOHN SAT on the end of his bed, dressed in a towel. He stared across the room where his service dress blues hung, freshly pressed from the dry cleaners. Five rows of medals, and he sat on the end of the bed and pressed his hands between his knees. His hands were shaking. His knees were shaking. He didn't deserve that Silver Star for conspicuous bravery. If he had an ounce of real honor, he'd snatch it off that uniform right now.

He'd had a dream the night before. He was a boy again, watching an old TV show. Chuck Connors had been an army man, falsely accused of cowardice. The drums started, the men standing in formation. Chuck marched in, and they'd stripped him of his uniform, his rank, tore off his hat and buttons while he stood brave and silent. They took his sword, broke it, and threw the pieces into the dust. Then he walked out of the fort, and they closed the log doors against him, forever. But in the dream, John was a boy, watching himself. Watching as they pulled off everything that had ever meant anything to him, left him dressed in a tattered blue shirt. He went off into the wild desert, on foot, not even a horse. What had that show been called? *Branded*. That was it. John could remember the tune as clearly as if it was 1965.

What do you do when you're branded, marked with a coward's name?
What do you do when you're branded, and you know you're a man?

He'd had the dream before, lots of times, when he wondered what they would do to him, what they would do to Gabriel, if anyone knew their secret. He remembered this, remembered loving Gabriel so desperately, then having to leave him alone, off to their lonely separate bunks, falling asleep to this poisonous little dream. It hardened his heart just a bit. It wasn't right. They shouldn't have had to live like that. They'd deserved better.

Shit. He needed to calm way the fuck down. He wasn't going in to see the IG with tequila on his breath. He wondered if Kim or Billy might have a spare Valium in their bathroom? Or maybe Gabriel? No, not Gabriel.

He didn't think he could bear to look into a medicine cabinet shared by Kim and Billy. He closed his eyes, lay back on the bed, imagining. Pink nail polish, watermelon and green-apple lip gloss, God knows what kind of jewelry, what kind of condoms and lube. He would not be able to keep his cool, faced with clear evidence that his baby was having sex. Kim was so clearly not mature enough for responsible sex, when he kept falling in love for forty-eight hours at a time, and there was no one on the green earth who was good enough for him, anyway. And Billy? Billy needed a little cowboy chastity belt or a heavily armed bodyguard. Oh, God, he would end up seducing the bodyguard, and he would wear the little chastity belt with leather chaps, his tiny butt hanging in the wind. It would be his newest mask.

And Juan? What if John and Gabriel were thrown in jail? Juan would not be left with a single man to respect and look up to. He would grow up with his mother's bitter words in his ears and no men to love, and his masculine soul would be trampled. It would be drugs, maybe. No, he would avoid the drugs, join the Marine Corps, just so he could be around men who would not disappoint him. And the Marines would send Gabriel's baby off to war.

How could he keep them all safe if he was thrown into the brig, disgraced? Was he going to end up a fucking jailbird? They couldn't take his degrees away. He still had a PhD, an engineering degree. Would they let him teach? Somehow he didn't think leadership seminars would go over in prison. Or he might be training the Aryan

Nations to take over the government. Not what he had planned for his retirement career.

John sat up, took a long pull from the bottle of tequila. Screw it, the IG could think what they wanted. Other than the tequila, there was nothing in his stomach besides Pepto-Bismol. He lay back down on the bed, stared up at the ceiling, carefully checked from corner to corner. No cobwebs. Oh, God. He was Out. Of. Control. "Help."

Gabriel stuck his head into the bedroom. He had a towel around his waist, was wiping the last of the shaving cream from his smooth brown cheeks. He looked carefully at John, splayed out on the bed, the bottle of tequila in his fist. Gabriel started grinning. "I know what you need."

He started humming, a stupidly addictive tune, dancing a little in his towel.

"Oh, no. Not that."

"She's a very kinky girl, the kind you don't take home to mama."

"No. Not 'Super Freak'. That's gonna push me right over the edge."

Gabriel was swinging his ass, and he hit the play button on the CD player by the bed. "Come on, baby. Let's get the blood moving." He danced his way to the end of the bed, pulled John up by the hands, and wrapped him up in his big arms. He smelled like Gabriel, warm and spicy, cedarwood and orange and male skin. "Why do we need these towels?"

He pulled his off, tossed it to the end of the bed, then slid his fingers into the top of John's towel. John was already dancing to the music, unable to stop himself. "I'm starting to hate this song," he said, and did a tricky little spin. When he spun away, Gabriel pulled his towel off, threw it on the bed.

Gabriel reached out for his hand, spun him again. They were singing, Gabriel with evident enjoyment, John because he couldn't stop himself. Gabriel pulled him in close, and they were dancing belly to belly, hips swinging to a rhythm that could only have come out of 1981. "'She's a super freak, she's super freaky....'"

Kim came through the door, stumbled to a stop so suddenly that Billy piled into him from behind. Their mouths dropped open in unison, then Billy covered his mouth, started to giggle.

John pointed toward the door. "Out."

Kim blinked, turned around, and pushed Billy out the door. John heard him whisper, "Billy, quick! Get the cameras!"

John walked like an Egyptian over to the bedroom door, reached down, and turned the lock. "We may need to get a dead bolt."

Gabriel reached for the bottle of tequila. The next song was playing. He took a long swig. "'Might as well face it, you're addicted to love.'"

JOHN WAS back to himself by the time they took a taxi to the lawyer's office. Some dancing, some laughing, some love, and then lunch with his boys, listening to Kim's plan to get a fiber-optic scope with a camera to slip under his bedroom door. His wonderful life, full to overflowing.

Gabriel called the lawyer a shark with a grudge, and agreed with Mike they didn't have to like him. John felt weirdly dislocated driving onto the base, the airmen at the gate saluting him, standing at attention, then walking into the IG's office, with everyone snapping to attention when he passed. He felt like he was back home, but strangers were living in his house.

Gabriel leaned over his shoulder. "You can't go home again. Are any of these kids even legal drinking age? I don't think so." John looked back at him. His face was sorrowful, just a little angry. This was as hard for him as it was for John. Gabriel had joined the army when he was eighteen.

A young airman escorted them to a conference room. The table was set with water, and there was a coffee mess in the corner. The airman fixed their coffee, giving John admiring looks from under her lashes. She handed him a cup, smiling. "I hope I can take your graduate seminar in leadership next semester, General. I'm nearly finished with my master's in history at UNM." He wondered how Johnny Cash had felt when he'd been thrown into the clink, and the deputies had asked him for an autograph.

He took his coffee, sat down next to Gabriel at the table. Gabriel had overheard. "I wonder if you're going to have time to teach a graduate seminar? In between watching the basil grow?"

"I've been wondering about that myself."

Gabriel gave his knee a squeeze under the table.

The young woman who came into the room caused the lawyer-shark to sit up and take notice. She was a beauty, dark hair cut in a bob and big dark eyes; an elegant figure in her service dress blues. John thought she looked vaguely familiar, wondered if he'd come across her in his last years in service, when she must have been a baby lieutenant. She was wearing captain's stripes now. She put down the folders she was carrying, made her way to their side of the long table, and shook hands. "General Mitchel, I'm Captain Curtis." She turned to Gabriel, studied him for a long moment. She glanced back at John for a moment, smiling, her dark eyes wide with appreciation. Gabriel was a very handsome man in his dress uniform.

You have no idea, John thought. *You haven't seen him in a flight suit*. John looked at Gabriel's glum face. The shark had told them it would be a bad sign if the IG gave them a woman or a junior officer. And Curtis was both. She was still standing. "General, gentlemen, I wonder if you would indulge me for a moment?"

The shark was already shaking his head.

She touched John briefly on the sleeve. "Sir, I have an old friend in my office who would like to say hello to you and CW-5 Sanchez before we begin. Would you mind?"

John could use all the old friends he could get. Something about her dark eyes, the shape of her face. Who did she remind him of? "Yes, of course." He looked at Gabriel. He was studying her as well, his bottom lip caught between his teeth.

They walked down the hall, and she pushed open the door to a typical military office: green metal desk, computers with a wild tangle of electrical cords underneath, standard-issue metal venetian blinds on the windows. She had a small pot of African violets on the window sill, and the violets were trying hard to bloom, one tiny purple flower reaching for the sun. The man sitting next to the desk stood when they

187

walked in. He had dark hair and eyes, like her, and a smile that lit up the room. He was dressed in jeans and a white button-down oxford hanging loose. He looked at them both, and John remembered a small, dusty boy, lips cracked from the heat, feet bleeding in his sandals, handing him a letter. Begging him to help his father. "Abdullah!"

He was laughing now, and crying, and his sister ducked out of the office to give them some privacy. He went into Gabriel's arms first, hugged him, and then John held him and stroked the dark hair. "You look so much like your father when I first knew him. Tell me how he is. I haven't spoken to him since Thanksgiving."

"He's okay. Some pain, you know. Arthritis where the bones were broken. He says the pain is just to remind him he's still alive. He's hot on the trail of some papyrus fragments that are alleged to have parts of an unknown Egyptian-Greek story. He says to tell you to come visit him, see if you can help him translate the demotic."

Gabriel pulled up chairs, reached out for his hand. "Why are you so tall? Did you grow up while we weren't looking? I thought your dad was joking when he said you were at Julliard. I didn't think they let little boys play those big cellos."

"I'm in San Francisco now, at the Conservatory. I had to leave New York. It wasn't safe. It... it's been hard for us. Since 9/11."

John studied his beautiful Arabic face. "Abdullah al-Salim. You have a home with me, anytime you want one. I hope you know that. How is San Francisco?"

"Weird. Cool. When I first arrived, the other guys in the strings section of the orchestra gave me a tee shirt that said 'I Only Look Like A Terrorist'. San Francisco humor. I knew I had found my place. Some parts of the country, wearing that tee shirt would get me shot."

Captain Curtis stuck her head back into the room. "Your lawyer is rumbling like a volcano about to blow. Do you want to get our business done, and then maybe we can all go out to dinner?"

John sighed, nodded. Gabriel gave Abdullah another hug. Told him to not disappear while they were being grilled by the lawyers. Abdullah pulled out his phone. "I'll find us someplace to eat. Someplace with green chili."

"Every restaurant in New Mexico serves green chili."

"Good. I'll start there." He looked up for a moment. "General? How's Kim? Is he around?" John noted with interest that Abdullah's cheeks were flushing with beautiful color.

Captain Curtis shook her head. "We can talk later. We're going to the Officer's Club. Surf and turf tonight. They grill a decent steak." She pointed at her brother's shirt. "Can you tuck that in? Just a little?" Abdullah just grinned at her. The sight of his happy face, all grown up, and John felt something in his chest that reminded him of the way Christmas morning used to feel when he'd been a kid. And he remembered Kuwait, in 1990.

He reached for Gabriel's sleeve when they were out of the office. "Thank you," he said.

"For what?"

"For always having my back. I was just remembering."

"Me too. That was a close one, my God. Let's not do that again, okay? I'm getting too old." He bent over, gave John a little nudge. "Hey, when did Kim and Abdullah meet? Was it that Christmas Kim was seventeen? You were in Cambridge that year, right?"

John shook his head. "I don't remember. I have a feeling there's a story I haven't heard. Do I want to hear it? We'll get Abdullah to spill the beans tonight. If we're, you know… not incarcerated."

Gabriel bent over and whispered in his ear. "If you ask one more lost boy to move into the house, I'm going to start building a barracks in the back yard."

John felt the color creep up his neck.

They followed Captain Curtis down the hall to the conference room. Which daughter was she? Omar had three, and if he remembered correctly, one was in London, married. Was this the little one, the baby his wife had carried in her arms out of Kuwait? No, couldn't be. He tried to do some math in his head, but gave it up, too stressed to carry a linear thought. She must be married, since she had a different last name than her father.

She turned to stop them before they went into the room. "Can I ask you something, General Mitchel? This is just for my own curiosity. Stories become legends, and then over time the facts get blurred. You're a legend in my family. Abdullah, he was never in the military, so I don't think he ever understood what he said you did, what my father said you did. But I'm in the army. I want to know the truth, not the legend. You were a general officer. Did you really go into enemy-controlled territory with an Apache helicopter and a couple of rifles and one pilot as backup? In the first days of a war, to rescue a civilian?" She studied their faces. "What were you thinking? What were you planning to do if you'd been captured?" She narrowed her eyes, looking carefully into both of their faces. "Okay, that's what I thought. That's exactly what you did." She grinned at him, then, shaking her head. "Unbelievable. General, they should have court-martialed you!"

She opened the door to the conference room, waited for them to be seated before she pulled out the chair at the head of the table. "Would anyone like more coffee?" John shook his head. Could this day get any stranger? "Gentlemen, are you familiar with the quote 'revenge is a confession of pain'? I believe that is the case with this deposition. The allegations were presented without foundation in factual evidence, and this deposition appears to constitute nothing more than hearsay and a cry of pain. The office of the inspector general is not able to use scant resources looking for that evidence, nor do we have any desire to do so. We have no evidence of a crime, and the allegations of behavior unbecoming an officer are, in the case of General John Mitchel and CW-5 Gabriel Sanchez, without basis in fact. We will not pursue any legal or administrative action based on the allegations in this deposition, now or in the future." She looked at Gabriel. "Sir, you have a plan for the care of your family?"

"Yes, I do."

"Your word will suffice. I am very sorry for the pain your family, and you both, have suffered. But as far as the army is concerned, your honor and your reputations are intact." She turned to the lawyer, who was studying her with a bemused look on his face. "A pleasure," she said, holding out a hand. "Thank you for coming."

When he'd left the room, she held out her hand to John, and he took it, feeling her firm grip. He thought she might work out boxing in the base gym. "I'm Amira," she said, taking pity on him. Could she tell he was still trying to calculate her age? "The middle daughter. I took my husband's name last year after we got married. Safer, that way, though the army is probably the safest place in the country for an Arab-American woman." She looked back at Gabriel, then smiled at him. "The IG looked for an advocate who had reason to admire and respect General John Mitchel to handle this matter. And they found me."

"They must have had to search long and hard."

"Not really." She squeezed his hand and let it go. "The way I heard it, we were lining up for the job. Your fans are legion, General. Sabers were rattling on your behalf all the way up Pennsylvania Avenue."

She held out an arm for Gabriel, and he escorted her back down the hall. "So, tell me all about that weird-ass law firm you work for. I heard you're doing 30 percent pro bono, but I know that's not true."

"Fifty percent," he admitted. "Sometimes more. Immigration, hate crimes, housing discrimination, mostly. We're lucky if we can cover the rent and the electric bill."

"I interned with the ACLU after law school. But I had those student loans to pay off."

"How close are you to paying them off?"

"It's done. I need to start looking around for my post-army career. I only have six months left at my current duty station."

"Where are you stationed?"

"Germany." She grinned at John's stunned look. "I was happy to have a quick trip home, to check on Father. And I haven't seen Abdullah since he went to San Francisco. Dinner is on me."

EPILOGUE

JOHN LEANED over the side of the basket, saw the ground fall away as swiftly as a bird's flight. It didn't feel like they were moving at all; there was just a soft warm breeze against his face and the earth falling beneath them. He looked up. Gabriel was wearing his flight suit, reaching over his head to make an adjustment to the airflow to the balloon. The fire made a soft, whooshing sound, but otherwise it was quiet, the movement of the basket so gentle it didn't feel like flight at all.

"What do you think?"

John smiled at him, leaned back against the basket. "After all this time you can still surprise me."

"I'm starting to crave the quiet," Gabriel said. "Maybe time changes us. I used to love the speed. Now I long for the peace of this kind of flight. The way I've always longed for you, from somewhere deep in my soul."

"Gabriel…."

"Only one thing hasn't changed, not in all this time."

John looked up at the balloon over his head. "I can't see it from here."

"Kim was supposed to take a picture and send it to my phone when we inflated." Gabriel pulled the phone out of his pocket, scrolled down with his thumb. "Is he really spending the day with Mike Adams, learning how to trim bonsai? Do you think Mike understands how wildly enthusiastic he gets?"

"Mike's the same way. He says he has over three hundred bonsai now, plus another hundred babies in plastic pots, ready to start training. He's talking about growing trees from seeds. I mean, that's a long-term project for your retirement years."

"The backyard is going to be overrun. I'm going to have to build something to hold them all. Kim was talking about a bonsai quince. I don't even know what a quince is. What's the matter with him, he doesn't want to fly in a balloon? And Billy claims to be afraid of heights? Couple of pansy-asses. Oh, look. Here it is." He turned the phone to John, and a golden horse rose from the side of their balloon, fierce, tangled black mane, wild black eyes.

"That looks like Genghis Khan's horse. I remember when you had that horse on the nose of your chopper."

John studied him from his side of the basket. Gabriel leaned back, grinned at him. They might tip over if they didn't keep their weight balanced. It would be a long way down to the ground. But Gabriel in a flight suit was nearly impossible to resist. John took a step forward, and Gabriel reached for his hand.

"Thank you for flying with me."

"Always. Thank you for watching my back."

"It has been my pleasure, General. Are you ready? For whatever comes next?"

"You and me? Kids and ex-wife? Our beautiful life. Should be an adventure."